Other works by the author:

Drinking of Spirits, stories
Goya's Head, novel
A Bad Piece of Luck, novel

Yonder Where the Road Bends

Tom Abrams

Livingston Press
The University of West Alabama

Copyright © 2018 Tom Abrams
All rights reserved, including electronic text
ISBN 13: 978-1-60489-217-8, hardcover
ISBN 13: 978-1-60489-216-1, trade paper
Library of Congress Control Number: 2018947852
ISBN: 1-60489-216-1, trade paper
ISBN: 1-60489-217-X, hardcover
Printed on acid-free paper
Printed in the United States of America by
Publishers Graphics

Hardcover binding by: HF Group
Typesetting and page layout: Sarah Coffey
Proofreading: Joe Taylor, Jane Duke
Cover layout: Sarah Coffey

This is a work of fiction. Any resemblance
to persons living or dead is coincidental.
Livingston Press is part of The University of West Alabama,
and thereby has non-profit status.
Donations are tax-deductible.

first edition
6 5 4 3 3 2 1

Yonder Where the Road Bends

—for Jane

1865
Tallahassee
Early March

Saturday evening. Smell of wood smoke from many houses. I am walking to the train depot. On the corner of 100 Foot Street, there is a gnarled old mulberry tree. In late spring the fruit will ripen, the first to do so around here, and I think fondly of Ma's mulberry pie.

I'd spent most the day wandering the countryside. I came across a little tumbledown school house out there, by a creek near a stand of oranges withered by cold long passed. It was one room, built of scantling pine, the thatch roof caved in and overgrown by grapevine and trumpet creeper. There was a doorway with no door, two open windows, one cut in the north side, one the south. It tilted badly. It was bare inside but for a homemade chalkboard, a piece of wood planed smooth and painted black. I put a finger to the board and wrote my name in the grime:

Virgil Hill

I made it as a token of some sort, tho' I did not know of what it might portend.

There was a fire in a barrel outside the depot, the old man who watched the place at night whittling a stick into a point nearby. Three men shooting craps by the light of a pine torch on the other side of the tracks. I'd hoped to meet up with a girl, but did not see her. So I was just standing around with my hands in my pockets. The next event of the evening might be to find a wall to lean against. But then I heard a rumble in the distance—the sound of a locomotive hammering along the rails. It is 9:00 o'clock. There are no night trains. Yet its whistle started up and kept on. This would turn out to be a special train. No freight or passengers. It was carrying news.

Yankee troops had landed on the coast near St. Marks lighthouse, 21 miles distant. A raid was in progress. They were headed our way.

I was then a military student at the West Florida Seminary. In two days, on Monday the 6th of March, I would take part in a fight against the Yankees at what became known as the Battle of Natural Bridge. A week later I would turn 17. But I mark the time when that locomotive rumbled into the depot, its big head-lamp burning. My life started to change right there.

General Sam Jones was the Confederate commander of the District of Florida. He had gone to West Point, an artillery man, made his rank at Manassas. He had an affection, it was told, for John Barleycorn. Many did. It was not something to be held against him. A good soldier withal, but he throve now on planning, organization. Brigadier General William Miller, second in command, was his field officer. Miller was infantry, also West Point and a Mexican War veteran. He had been in Florida since January of '63, recovering from a wound suffered at Murfreesboro, Tennessee.

The two needed to muster all available men in Middle Florida. Cannon started signaling the planters and home guards in the area. Couriers rode to surrounding hamlets, and telegraphs were sent to Marianna and from there on to southern Georgia. Word went eastward to Madison and Lake City, northwest to Quincy. The generals wanted rolling stock—locomotives, freight cars, soldiers. They wanted horsemen. They wanted folks with guns and in a hurry.

Men and boys of all stamp responded. They would gather at the train depot in the coming hours, throughout the night, and the next day. One of these, a deserter named Neil Clary, would for a short time enter my life and become important to it long after.

The next morning was raw, a cold wind sawing from different angles. It was still so at noon as we assembled at school and marched to the Capitol building, where we were sworn into Confederate service. Then our principal, Captain Valentine Johnson, marched us to the train depot. Once there, the Captain informed the youngest they would not be going along. They were to stay back with him. My little buddy, Egg Nims, was one of these. He was sore about it, but he was only 11.
General Miller and his staff, our company of cadets, and a band of old milish from Quincy in Gadsden County, called the Silver Grays, crowded into boxcars with scattered pine straw to sit on. The train carried us south to Wakulla Station. It was my first train ride. Not so long ago there were no engines on this line. Mules pulled cars full of cotton bales, tobacco. Mules are more my speed. I was still rocking and swaying for a time after we got out of the thing. Took awhile for to get its motion out of me.
From Wakulla we marched six miles to the village of Newport and on to the bridge over the St. Marks River. We got there late in the afternoon and took up positions.

Newport

Lt. Colonel George Washington Scott was in command at Newport. He had 100 rifles, made up of his men from the 5th Florida Cavalry Battalion, marine and artillery personnel. The artillery had lost their gun the previous day, a brass 12-pounder, in a fight at the bridge over East River—which wound through the marsh near the lighthouse. The 12-pounders are deadly at close range, and that was a loss. Scott's men had skirmished off and on since. They were badly outnumbered, kept falling back. At the Newport Bridge they made a stand.

Colonel Scott is from Tallahassee. We knew him. He had been to our classes, read from *Benn's Tactics*, a cavalry book he'd learned from. I remember his brass spurs clinking as he strutted around the classroom. He, at the moment, looked spent.

Throughout the evening, more of our cavalry arrived.

Captain Lee Butler, an aide to General Miller, was attached to us. He would stay on with us at Natural Bridge. We had our own cadet Captain, John Wesley Wethington. He was the oldest of us, nearly 18. He had enlisted in the home guard the year before and fought at Olustee Station. He was well thought of. We had a cadet 1st Lieutenant and a 2nd that no one thought of one way or the other about. We also had new blood, boys who had enlisted with us that day, including John Milton, the 15-year-old son of the Governor, and Will Rawls, who I had not met before but he would spend the fighting at my side. Along the river, we were shot at for the first time—shot back.

Scott's men had set fire to the east end of the wooden bridge, one bay gone there now, and dismantled the west end. A saw mill, grist mill, and foundry on the east side of the river had been torched as well so Yankee troops could not use them for cover. The fire was still burning. Scott left a small detachment of videttes on that side to scout. Earthen entrenchments were already in place on our side, built the previous year by conscripted slaves at General Miller's direction. They extended several rods above and below the bridge.

I had been to Newport once before. My uncle Jerome bought an ox here several years ago, and I went along with him. He was Pa's oldest brother, 12 years between their ages, and about ready for a cowbell himself. I was there to keep an eye on him. I recalled the town bustling, two hotels, a cotton mercantile, cotton bales piled on the docks, tobacco and salt warehouses, picket fences around the houses and lemon trees in the yards. I recalled also the river's clarity. Springs feed into it here. But the water now high from winter rains, ran rough and tumble.
    We saw black soldiers over on the other side. It was a novelty, and but for John Wesley, the first time any of us had ever seen a negro with a gun.
    Firing continued back and forth through twilight, musketry spitting, deliberate and sporadic. After dark the shooting quit.

Cadets had matching uniforms but our rifles were unspecific. The gun I carried once belonged to my father. He had used it in war. It was older than me, a Springfield .69 caliber smooth-bore musket, accurate to 50 yards or so when my eye was true, tho' I never had to kill anything that far away except a target.
    The weapon was familiar to me. I took many deer with it, hog. I could shoot the head off a turkey. I had never shot at armed game before. I fired, got down, reloaded. Not at all sure I hit anything, probably not. Most important to me, I was cautious but not in any way rattled.

When we first got to the bridge, the Yankee cannon were throwing shells. Their gunners kept firing high, the loads thudding into the village to our rear. Metal searing the air has a quavering shriek to it. That was the first time I heard it coming at me. Shortly thereafter they switched to canister, a bunch of one-inch cast iron balls, like big shotgun blasts. Same results. The village took the brunt of it.

At dark, we built low fires down in the trenches at different spots along our line. Rations were salt bacon and cornmeal. This was supposed to last three days but did not take into account nervous hunger. I found it short fare. I fried the two together with a little water and made cush, ate it through the night and not much left over. We huddled against each other for warmth, blankets over our shoulders, oilcloths over them, trying for comfort but hard to come by.

We had been tried by fire now and, from what I heard, tales of it were being perfected—a truthful element included here and there, well dusted with bullshit. There were rumors afloat. We furthered them. They kept sparking, but there was not enough truth in them to catch. We traded off sentry duty throughout the night. Odor of burnt wood from across the bridge, ash in the air.

I had not noted any livestock their side of the river. Mules like to bray. I had not heard that. No horses snorting. I distinctly heard the Yankees hitching up over there but to what was a mystery. We found out later they used a company of troops to push and drag their field pieces—moved them by hand. Hitched rope to guns and caissons and, howsomever you figure it, no easy task. They had not brought any beasts.

From that side, we started hearing Cracker parlance and pronunciation. One of our Gadsden County men, a grizzled Indian fighter, recognized the croaking drawl of an old neighbor across the way.

Frog Reeves? That you o'er there cussin'?

Who wants to know? came the answer. You had to cup an ear with your hand to get what was said from that side.

Burtis Crowder.

The one they call Big Ugly?

One an' the same. Tho' I think it wrongly coined. I am more handsome of late.

I'll not believe that. Show your face.

Not gone happen, Burtis said. I ain't stupid.

Since when?

Burtis said, You still hangin' with that mean set you use to?

What mean set?

Your brothers.

Sharp crack of a rifle from that side—minnie ball cutting the air overhead. It made a sound like *izzt*.

The two old neighbors exchanged insults across the river a bit more, some good-natured in that dry humor and raillery the old troopers favored, some not. Frog admitted to being pie-eyed. They had come across a hogshead of scuppernong wine. Burtis Crowder knew already what outfit Frog had signed on with, the 2nd Florida Union Cavalry. That's who the white troops were over there. They were Florida men, Federal sympathizers, horse thieves, marauders, whiskey heads, three companies of them we found out later.

I saw a flame ignite over a pipe there. I was about to pull down on it, but then reconsidered—Hell, let the man have a smoke.

Throughout the night, local patriots joined us with their weapons.

When we were shooting and getting shot at in return, I did not fret over that I might get hurt. No man that goes into battle but has his fears. I felt excitement, I know, and would guess fear played a part in that. It is said if you are not scared some, you are most likely a fool. The excitement, tho', coursed through me. From time to time it would rush up the back of my head.

At some point across the river, the Yankee troops began a night march. We heard sounds there, a general bestirring—the clank of artillery harness, rattle of wheels, axles calling out for grease, low talk like the sound of distant bees—for what purpose we could not know. But our scouts on that side got word back across. Colonel Scott and three companies of cavalry left to shadow the Yankee movements along our side of the river and to block a possible ford near Tompkin's Mill, three miles upriver from Newport. The river was swollen there and past crossing, and the Yankees continued on. Scott sent this information on to Tallahassee, and General Sam Jones then directed our forces to converge on Natural Bridge, the next dry crossing. Couriers galloped into our position at Newport Bridge, galloped away on their errands. It is worthy of remark, and I have not done so yet, that there was at the time no telegraph between Tallahassee and the coast. Not to the wharf at St. Marks or to Newport either.

I was relieved of sentry duty soon after 3:00 a.m. It was my second posting, four hours off in between, during which I stayed awake. I sat down by one of the fires that had gone to ember and closed my eyes to rest them. They felt terribly bloodshot. I awoke in short order to the low rumble of cannon fire in the distance. The guns echoing sounded like as of a horse galloping across an old plank bridge far off in the night. Eight miles away, the fight at Natural Bridge had begun. I had slept an hour, maybe less.

Near daybreak, we took a shot across the river to make sure our weapons were dry. No response from the other side but for grumbling.

A Gadsden man said, Look thar. What is that reckoned to be?

What he pointed out was a bony white ass. One of the Yankees was taking a shit near a big live oak. It was not hard to spot him. He was leisurely finishing up his business and seemed unconcerned with life or limb.

That is pure cussedness, he said.

Load up, said another.

And they aimed and fired. Lead must have punched about him over there, but when the smoke cleared we saw him, in the same unconcerned manner, hitching up his galluses. Then he gave us the finger and disappeared from view.

Natural Bridge

So we had a laugh about that. And then we began the march to Natural Bridge. We moved along the west side of the river on the Newport Plank Road. Half the road was plank, the other half slush. Locals took over the trenches at Newport to hold in place the Yankee soldiers remaining. The Yanks left the white troops there, took their negro troops on to Natural Bridge. I never rightly understood that, tho' it is possible those boys were not sober enough to make it to work.

I was listless when we began the march. By the time we neared the battlefield at 8:30 that morning, I was borderline crazy with energy.

We stopped once, what turned out to be a mile from the battle line, at the field hospital. Two cadets were left there to help. I was pleased not to be included. The hospital was a canvas top held up by sapling poles, a no sides open affair with a table in the middle. The table looked to be a barn door. It rested on sawhorses. There were bone saws, bullet probes and the like on display, wounded men bandaged and in discomfort, surgeons in blood-stained aprons. Colonel J. J. Daniels, in charge of the 1st Florida Reserves, was there all banged up. During a skirmish early on, his horse shied at cannon fire and bolted sidelong into a pine tree. The Colonel was trying to move around a little and not doing any good at it.

I watched one of the surgeons sharpening a scalpel. A twitch soon started below my left eye that would come and go throughout the day. The little muscle twitching was before then unknown to me.

During the previous night, our reinforcements from Tallahassee had traveled on the railway, a quarter-mile train with engines in front and back, got out at the turpentine camp near Woodville after midnight, a place called Old Still, and marched on to Natural Bridge. They arrived at the bridge around 4:00 a.m. They had formed a sickle moon defensive line, the size of which extended down close to the river above and below the bridge. It allowed converging fire at the point where the Yankees had to cross. Two Yankee advances had been stayed early on. We learned this from the artillerymen posted nearby us. According to them, the first of these had been a damned dog fight. The second wore along but was merely hard work. That skirmishing had woken me back in Newport.

At the battle line, we stacked arms, unslung our knapsacks, drew entrenching tools. There were several old earthworks around left over from a stockade fort built during the 1st Seminole War, the wood of the fort gone now to time and weather. We were placed at one of these. Captain Butler staked out how he wanted it improved. The works needed to get so that, aiming over the top, we would not be exposed below our shoulders. Keep it between you and the hurt he told us.

You're hit, he said, that most likely will be in the forehead. You will not recall it.

We looked around at each other on that one, then got to it at a right smart pace, plying spades and bayonets and bare hands. We'd trade off if need be—some at rest while others worked. The earthen wall got taller, the trench behind it deeper. We worked till the Captain was satisfied with the job. Then we waited.

We were positioned just to the left of the Natural Bridge road where the road crossed the battleline. Our works formed a shape that poked out from the line like a horseshoe, what the military call a salient. To our right were Captain Patrick Houstoun's two guns from the Kilcrease Light Artillery. They could fire directly down the road. I was at the far right of our salient, Will Rawls beside me, Charlie Ellis next in line, Del Olney next to him, and further along, Bobby Ledsmith.

We looked toward the crossing.

What they doin' o'er there? Will said.

All them gunboats, Charlie said, got to be a heap more troops on the way. They jes' waitin' on 'em.

Maybe they ain't half so many as we think, I said.

I bet they boilin' coffee, Del said. Store coffee.

I clean forgot the taste a that, Charlie said.

Buster Pruitt wandered down our way just then. Buster is twice as big as the rest of us, in width anyway. Buster is a slowpoke, would best describe him I think. And he is working toward slug. He was wanting to know if we had any rations left. If there were any, it was not revealed.

He stayed to chat a little, tho' no one had yet spoken to him.

I'm hungry, he said.

So'm I, Del said.

I was talkin' with the Cap'n, Buster said, spoken like he and Cap might have been discussing tactics.

About what? Charlie said.

He told me when the fightin' starts, I should *pull it taut*. Then after he said it, he laughed.

Pull it taut? Bobby Ledsmith said.

Yeh, Buster said. Not sure what that meant. But … why did he laugh?

He ain't have to do that, Charlie said.

I thought not, Buster said.

I'd like ta see the man as did! Charlie said. He liked to jerk Buster's chain.

Buster studied Charlie a bit, then began dawdling back to his spot along the works.

A moment later Will said, Nigh as I can come at it, the Cap's talkin' about that big un's arsehole. What you say his name be?

Buster.

Hey Buster, Will called out. Pucker up, man!

Buster looked back with an expression on his face asking *What in hell they all goin' on about this morning?*

Captain Dunham had arrived at 9:00 with three additional cannon from the Milton Light Artillery. One of these was set to the far left side of our line, hard by a cypress slough, and the other two along the right flank where Lt. Whitehead's detachment of Gadsden County milish had already positioned their single cannon.

Six field pieces of various caliber had now been planted as on a chess board along an arcing defensive line. They would allow us to pepper the bridge and ground between with direct and crossfire of canister and grapeshot.

On our left flank, Lt. Colonel Girardeau of the 1st Florida Militia commanded a force of home guard companies from five counties. Neil Clary was among them, I knew, but fit in so well I could not spot him. Girardeau's men were rough-hewn, long beards, chaw spitters. Just on the whole, they looked a cantankerous lot. They understood naught of spit and polish but knew their weapons well. They were used to killing prey with bad dispositions—bear, panther, wolf, boar. I studied them a bit, many in winter buckskins, taking in the scene, the distances, on the hunt.

The right flank was formed by the entire 1st Florida Reserves, 6, 7 companies of them. I noted raw kids there, saw gray-locks men. The line was extended on around to the river's edge by three companies of dismounted soldiers from the 5th Florida Cavalry under Major William Milton, along with Captain Ben Chaires' company of home guards from Leon County. The Major was another of the Governor's sons. His pickets had first spotted the Yankees on the coast and were the first to engage them.

A dense hammock covered the crossing and extended

out from it some—live oak, magnolia, white ash, beech, pignut hickory, cabbage palm, sweetgum, bay. There were sloughs and thickets surrounding the river. In the swamp areas, bald cypress were still winter stark with moss tresses hung long. They looked in mourning. When the density gave way, it did so to slash pine, sawtooth scrub. There were many pines around, both standing and fallen, that our men made use of for cover and built entrenchments amongst.

We were not in a large area. There were a lot of men contained in it. We had the high ground, tho' it was hardly steep—more a gradual decline to the bridge. It might have looked a bit more elevated from the Federal viewpoint, maybe like a hillock to them. We could not see the river where we were but knew its course and nature. Most of us had camped here, fished. If you drew a straight line on a map, the bridge was nine miles from Tallahassee.

There was another side to the place hard to dismiss. Redbud were blooming all around. Swamp maple wingnuts had just popped out, bright red in color. Yellow jessamine with its sweet smell crowned bushes and trees. Winter grasses shown pecan brown and sorrel. Wild grapevines hung down, so thick you could not fit two hands around them. It was a tangled wilderness, as it had always been, and a pretty one.

The Yanks were 150 yards away when they charged, give or take. Until then we had not seen them. We were approaching on 1,000 troops strong and more on the way. We knew but little of how many they had hither.

Tallahassee:

I must now go backwards some. Like I said earlier, I ran into Neil Clary Saturday night at the train depot. I was there because I wanted to meet up with a girl who lived nearby. I happened to be at the depot also because there was little else to do. Saturday night you would try your best, as Sunday it all closed down but for the churches. Tallahassee, even tho' the state capital, was no more than a big country town on the frontier. Atlanta's population before Sherman got to it was 10,000 or so. Tallahassee then not 2,000, and nearly half slaves. It was a place both charming and rough.

There was big money in the local banks. Cotton plantations surrounded the town, owned by gentlemen farmers who existed in a world much more high-runged than the rest of us. The planters owned two-thirds of the land around Tallahassee, and all the good land. They were descendants of the Mayflower, of old Virginia, the Carolinas and Georgia cotton and tobacco gentry, of Washington and Jefferson. Even, for a time, a nephew of Napoleon was included in that number. He died when I was but little. The plantation carried on. When the Frenchie cotton wagons come to town, the mule teams decorated with bells high up on their hames, the streets turn melodic.

The town had a hard side. To my way of thinking there were way too many lawyers, most the two-penny sort. They could be hired out of various taverns. There was gambling, ladies of the night strolling down Adams and Monroe, hog and cattle pens in the town limits, chickens pecking in the streets. And the horseshit in the streets matched only by that found in sessions of the legislature. They had recently passed a law renaming brothels *houses of ill fame*. It became a joke around town. No one knew quite what that meant. It did not stop a number of the lawmakers from frequenting them.

The town was situated on one of the many red clay hills in the area. Sea Island cotton did well in the clay. The Capitol stood over other structures in its grandeur—a two-story stuccoed-brick building with a heavy-columned portico. If you built in town now it had to be constructed of brick, slate roof, this to discourage fire, but there were many firetraps still around. The fire of 1843 had destroyed most everything, and there were still empty lots in the center of town as reminders of it. There were several large inns. Boarding houses. Any number of saloons, most of the wrong sort.

I thought the main building of our seminary, located on the west end of Clinton, impressive. Built of brick covered by cement painted white, two stories, with the front porch supporting four tall columns, it had the look of a Greek temple. It sat on a rise known as Gallows Hill, once used for hangings.

There was a thriving business district of connected shops—mercantile, saddler and harness, barber, dry goods, apothecary, wheelwright, good horse troughs along it, and then and again a hitching post or mounting block. Heyward's Grocery and Produce was there, Slusser's Hardware, and others, including a book store, dressmaker, gunsmith. Little shops scattered here and there on the side streets—butcher, tailor, blacksmith, livery stable. There was a cabinet maker named Tulk who also made canes, and coffins of cypress or pine. The streets were shaded by centenary oaks, magnolia, cedar. If the blockade-runners made it through at St. Marks, the stores would have goods in them.

We had our own brewery that supplied the saloons, and sometimes, when the weather was fair on market day and the brewer amiable, he would push a little beer cart around Rascal's Square. His sociality depended entirely on how early in the morning he'd begun sampling his goods. There were some especially raw whiskey shops down the alleys that folks referred to as doggeries. Their whiskey was inexpensive and could all but blister you on the way down.

There were some fine houses set back on large lots, especially on Calhoun Street, a number of them constructed by a master builder in the '30s, John Proctor, a free negro. The women of the town were rightly proud of their gardens, their roses and crepe myrtle and japonicas.

In times of quiet around here, the stagecoach brings mail to town twice a week. The schedule tended to get interrupted of late. The stage drops a bag of mail at the post office and passengers at Brown's City Hotel, Planters Hotel. It is sort of an event. If you were downtown when the stage came in, you took notice. There was a sense that it brought the world along with it.

There once was a race track north of town my Pa thought much of, a circled mile, a judges' stand and betting rooms. In the old days, each December, a derby took place during a four-day stretch. Pa faithfully attended these. I stop there on my walks now, the track and everything about it gone to memory, try to imagine him placing a bet, excited about a horse he liked. But for race time tho', he was so close-fisted with his money I have some trouble picturing it.

The area has become a favorite for duels. There are Tallahassee ways to these. Pistols, the participants back to back at 10 paces, one shot each. At the command *Wheel* they would turn and fire. If both happened to miss, they handed over their guns to the seconds, then closed on each other with Bowie knives. The seconds were well-armed and more than ready to get involved should anyone try to interfere in the drama. The practice was illegal and a hefty fine long on the books, but no one paid any attention to it, including the Law.

The town had a bustle to it when the politicians were in session. Otherwise, in the evening, you are liable to see a dog asleep in the middle of any thoroughfare. A stray cow might wander past you. And it was not out of the way to find a rich planter's son drunk in French Town with some doxie, acting foolish, or worse. The place was small enough that you got to know everybody to one degree or another, and some that you did not at all want to.

I would go by the depot Saturday nights to meet up with that girl. She was a couple years older than me, a wild sort, which I liked about her. She had a smile that never seemed to fit right until she took a drink. She near always had a snuff stick protruding from her lips. I did not find the habit attractive, but she had some attributes that let you dismiss it. We'd meet up or not. It depended on if she could get away.

I did not see her, but I noticed Neil Clary. He had been shooting craps with two other men. Then all the excitement halted the game.

Neil stood out. He wore a colorless slouch hat, a faded and soiled gray jacket, homespun jeans gone ragged, and had no shoes. He was tall, maybe 6 foot 2, broad-shouldered, with long hair and a wild red beard. I saw he had punched a number of holes in his belt. He wore a plain gold ring on his right hand. He looked a rough sort, to say the least, and tattered so he was close on to a vagabond. But he had a Bowie knife and carried a nice rifle, a Henry. It was, for the most part, used by Yankee cavalry, a lever-action repeating rifle. I had seen illustrations of these in a book, but this was the first I'd come across in person. He noticed me admiring it.

Here, boy, he said. Take a-holt of it.

The rifle felt good in my hands. He showed me how you would load it. There is a long loading sleeve, a 16-round tube magazine. He showed me how to fire. The lever had a slick action to it.

Holding the rifle, I was struck by something that had not occurred to me from the illustrations. The weapon had a 24-inch barrel—there was no wood on it. You just held on to metal with your left hand.

This barrel get hot? I said.

Yeh, it do, do you shoot it fast. What you need is a glove. I got it off one a Sherman's scouts. His glove would not fit. He had a daintier hand.

You killed him?

Well, I asked politely for the piece, but that did not set right with 'im.

But you did, I bet.

He might could have ducked, Neil said, had he any sense.

I held the weapon in the middle with one hand, palm up. It was perfectly balanced. And compared to my long gun, felt nearly a toy.

He showed me one of the .44 caliber slugs.

You need to get 'em close on to you, he said. Do so … an' this will light a man up. I shit you not.

I only got 12 cartridges, he said. There gone be a fight, think I'll come along, see can I find me some more. An' a pair a shoes, he added. A horse, if they have any. Or a mule would do, could I find one pleasant enough. Folks figure a mule is dumb and stubborn. I take 'em for a lot smarter than horses. They slow to do things, as they tryin' to work out jes' exactly the best way to fuck with you. An' do not be expectin' to fight white men, he added. What they'll send here is their nigras.

And except for some white officers, it turned out to be so.

How you know that?

I talked to the stoker, he said.

I told him about the seminary, that I was a student there. He asked could I write a letter for him, as he was not much good at it. He said who the letter was for, Ella Mayfield, and where she lived, a hamlet on the Manatee River.

Where about is that? I said.

Down below Tampa Bay. It's a settlement on the river's north side … bears no name yet and is not much account.

Three, four families, a general store, livery stable. The letter needs sent to Manatee, a village upriver some. They have a paddle boat landing there. An' a post office.

He took off the gold band and showed it to me. *Ella* was engraved on the inside.

I did some cow huntin' a couple years afore I got to fightin'. They call it the Cow Cavalry now. We ran cattle north for the Confederacy an' south for the Cuban market, down Punta Rassa way to the Cuban ships. There was money to be made down there. They paid in Spanish doubloons and silver. I gave Ella a couple doubloons one time, jes' souvenirs for her. I came around from a drive some time later, and she gave me this. He looked at the name a moment, then put the ring back on his finger. She knew a jeweler in New Orleans, he said, was kin to her I think. She is from there, he said, from New Orleans.

What you want said in the letter?

Tell her I'll be home soon as I get presentable. I'd not want to knock at her door and scare hell out a her. Say I'm takin' in the sunshine here in Tally, while my fine boots and broadcloth suit get fitted. I need to ask her if the oranges was any account ...

That all? You might want to romance it up a little.

Best not over-do it, he said. I have many things to tell her, and I'll do so in person here shortly. Hey, he said, that's good. Put that in it. An' tell her I got no card debts. She worries about shit like that for some reason.

I used to carry her image, he said, but it got destroyed in Georgia. A shell hit my tent. I was not in it but my gear was ... and her likeness.

I promised to write the letter, but because of what happened later on it would not get done.

When we had spoken for a time, he told me straightaway that he was a deserter, from the 7th Florida Volunteers, Army of Tennessee. He said he had been around Tallahassee for a couple days but stayed in the deep woods outside town, did not enter until near dark this night. He had walked here from north Georgia. That he walked what felt like forever and a day.

My Pa fought in the 3rd Seminole War, the Billy Bowlegs War it was called. He mustered into the militia for six months back then, but at the end of that time they wanted to keep him on. He was their best hunter. He discharged himself and came home, and the war continued on a year longer. He done wrong I guess, but I was pleased to have him back. So I had nothing to say to Neil Clary on the subject. I made no judgement. Folks do whatever they have to sometimes, regardless of what they are supposed to. I know for a fact my father was no coward, and I doubted Neil was either. After a while he would tell me just why he'd walked away.

He handed me a slip of paper, soiled, spilled upon, unfolded and creased again any number of times.

I am not so good at readin', he said. Would you take a look here?

He had been paroled, the document said, tho' the name there was different than his. Paroled at Vicksburg I told him—9 July 1863.

The Yanks stopped parolin' a while back, I said. Your name is Horst Mueller, by the way.

A Dutchman? he said.

He had come across the remains of a soldier along the Atlanta and West Point railroad tracks, back in some among the pines. He did not know if he was in Alabama by then or Georgia still.

Where I found him, he said, was out in the sticks. I figured he died of his wounds on the way home. Was no tellin' where he'd been hit. The critters had scattered him. Did not know where home was for him. I had a hunch 't was the Car'linas. Not sure why I thought it. Maybe he told me some way.

I gathered his bones an' covered him with rocks ... spoke some words over his grave. I said, I hope you are in God's country now. An' I could not think a nothin' else. I might a spoke about the weather a little. A sad service. I expect he deserved more.

I looked at his papers, he said. They were in a little crock was stopped with a corncob nubbin. There was a letter. I left that. Stamps.

He searched through his poke, found several stamps with Jeff Davis' likeness and handed them to me.

For my letter, he said. But tell me ... you think this will work? he said of the parole. Should they start askin' questions here? I had a feller ask me for papers in Alabama. He was nobody, jes' acted like he was big.

What happened?

I knocked his front teeth loose.

You do not look like a Horst, I said. You know any German?

Lager, he said, is Dutch, ain't it? Sauerkraut?

You ever been to Vicksburg?

Ne'r been to Mis'sippi.

How about medical leave?

Ne'r been wounded, he said. Not a scratch.

Ague?

Well now, I mean, folks along the river is got that, he said. Take some quinine, and bear with it. Quinine an' whiskey even better. Jes' part a life there. If it comes on, you go about shakin' for a couple weeks. The women all have these little Dr. Sappington's pills they swear by. But I've a mule's constitution. I've not cotched sick with nothin', except a cough or two.

You best go ahead and be Horst Mueller then if need be. An' do not tell anybody else what you told me, I said. How come you to say that?

He was in nowise put off by this. He was amused.

I ain't told another soul, he said. Anything else?

You cuss too much, I said.

That set him to laughing.

Trust me on this, I said. Get caught steppin' off, these boys here will put you down like a sick cur.

It will not happen, he said. I promise ye. He slapped me on the shoulder, grinned, and we walked on.

As it turned out, no one had time to look too closely at him just then. They needed gunmen. They needed hard cases. He fit the bill on both counts. We walked around town some looking for information. The warning cannon kept going off. The bell of the First Presbyterian Church tolled. Town folks were gathered with lanterns at the telegraph office seeking news. We walked down toward the Capitol building, where the military had set up a command post.

Across the street from the Capitol is City Hotel. It is a large, handsome old inn, partly brick and partly board, with long piazzas and a peaked roof, dormer windows. Their bar is lively I am told.

Neil said, Look-it that, referring to the hotel, and headed toward the front door.

Now they always have a guard stationed there. The guards in general are low-key but not to be fooled with. If they did not think you belonged to go inside, you most probably would not make it there.

I knew this particular guard, a man named Clement. He has a pronounced stoop, bent over enough to have kept him from the War. He was bent and bone lean, but I knew he carried a sap and was handy with it. He had some vinegar to him. Still, there were worse men in town. He took a quick survey of Neil and denied us entry.

Neil did not appear to be angered by this—he was grinning—more like a friendly bout might be in order, and he was up for it.

Whoa … hey! I said and grabbed his arm as he started to square off.

Virgil, Clement said, would you please get him gone.

You know him? Neil said.

Yeh, I do.

Oh, he said.

He nodded to Clement and turned around like none of this had ever happened.

Where was we headed to now? he said.

We came across a local I knew well, Earl Slusser. Slusser's Hardware has been around since I could remember. They had done business with Pa for years. Earl had dealings with the militias in the area as well. He was ancient when the War started and not fit for the ranks. He was a politician who would not think of running for office, one of those knew everyone and, at all times, what was going on in town. And he was an ardent Rebel. Even his eyes were Confederate gray. I heard told that, if you owed him money and were not inclined to repay promptly, those eyes would turn to ice and he would dun you without mercy till you settled with him.

I asked Earl if the cadets were going.

Aye, he said. Y'uns gone fight this time.

I told him Neil needed an outfit to join. He looked Neil up and down.

You want in on this?

I do.

Where you get that rifle? Earl said.

Kennesaw Mountain, Georgia.

We can use you then, he said. See can you find Colonel Girardeau and his home guards at the train depot. Tell 'im I sent you.

Do we get rations? Neil said.

Three days rations, what I heard.

We went to my quarters. I got my equipment together, knapsack, haversack, canteen. Checked my musket, cartridge box and belt, bayonet. I showed Neil my uniform.

We wear them during school, I said. We'll wear them tomorrow.

I had two hard-boiled eggs in my room that I gave to him. The day before, he had come across a runaway slave at a pond in the woods some miles west of town. He was a kindly old uncle and asked Neil to dine with him. He'd caught a nice catfish. The runaway was a wagoner and jack-leg carpenter at the plantation where he came from, but he had lived in the woods since the summer past. He looked well enough fed but was hungry for news. It marked the last time Neil had eaten.

I gave Neil a gum poncho I kept extra. It would keep him warmer than what he had and dry if it rained. After a while, we walked to the south end of town where descends a long steep hill leading into the countryside.

He looked into the dark there a moment or two and said, Could I borrow 10 cents for a beer?

Where might you get that?

Back there. He pointed to a hand-written sign out front of a tavern: Beer 10 cents—Whiskey 15.

The dice did not work out? I said.

Did fine for a while, he said. Then they stopped tumbling right. Was not like I was playin' with sharpers. The dice jes' turned on me. Could I found a billiards table, I would have cash in my pocket. There is no skill in craps. It is pure luck. I always considered myself a lucky man, but lately I have not had much.

I was under the impression you could not read.

I can read food an' drink, he said.

He searched his pockets.

I have nary a cent, he said.

I gave him a dime. It was an actual coin, not paper scrip, one I carried for years as a charm.

Seems a high price for a beer, I said.

He looked at the tavern in an admiring way.

I have cashed many a paycheck in such establishments, he said.

When he pulled open the door, a wealth of racket, pipe

smoke, stale beer and body stink rushed out. I stayed where I was on the street. One of the rules for cadets is that we are not allowed in Tallahassee saloons. But I knew this place. It was of mixed repute but swell if you were into knife fights. Neil came out shortly.

I had to drink it from a gourd, he said, but ... damn, it tasted jes' right.

We spent another three, four hours together at the depot as he waited for Colonel Girardeau. Folks from the area were gathering there, milling around or leaning on their muskets, greeting old friends long unseen. You might have took it for a country fair. There were bonfires. Hucksters peddling cigars, corn cakes, roasted sweet potatoes, boiled eggs, pickles. It was a rabble army assembling, a gathering of roughs, every pattern of man, boy and weapon in attendance.

I had not seen that many Bowie knives in one place before. The old Indian fighters favored them. I can only conjecture as to why. Another of the cadet rules—we are not allowed to carry Bowie knives in town. This was galling. It made no sense whatsoever. I have a Bowie knife that Pa gave me. I keep it at home. The firelocks and old time powder horns in the hands of country boys seemed relics of previous wars, no telling how far back. The uniforms on several of the very old gents from much fancier conflicts. No matter. All were willing.

At some point, Neil said, The fightin' gets sharp, I'll need to go off alone. I can do better work on my own.

I looked down at Neil's feet just then, the soles callused so they could be oak bark. The front of his breeches were scorched. I had seen this before on vets, from getting up next to campfires to keep warm. He had called me *boy*. During our time together I learned his story and that he was only three years older than me. It was hard to believe, as he was so worn.

You got any advice for me? I said. For tomorrow I mean.

Do not stand close to the cannon, he said.

Why is that?

They give you a headache.

After a while he said, You liable to be surprised at the noise and stink.

Stink?

The smoke, he said. Mostly from the cannon. It is the smell a brimstone.

A bit later he said, You takin' your old musket?

Yeh.

You bite enough a them paper cartridge, your tongue will turn blue. Do not worry on it.

He took a leather string out of his poke, a yard and some in length, and cut it in two, gave me half.

You hit in the arm or leg, tie it off quick. Or have someone else do it if you too fucked up. It might save ye.

I hope not to be hit, I said.

It happens, he said.

There was a hard frost on the ground by the time I got back to my quarters.

Natural Bridge

The bridge is made of limestone, six rods wide and so heavily wooded you could not see a thing in the timber there, just like looking into the dark. The St. Marks River here bends around an elbow crook to the west before turning south again where it drops into a sinkhole above the bridge and runs underground for a piece. The water rises and falls in a series of limestone sinks and swamp, rises at last in a basin where, after passing a ledge of rock, the river flows its course again. The old road curves as it comes off the bridge, the land built up some to its right.

This rise overlooks the crossing. It was vantage ground for Girardeau's gunmen. There is an open field, maybe 20 acres, maybe less, directly out from the crossing. It had been farmed previous but had not been tilled for a season or two. It was gone overgrown, thistle-choked, scrub palmetto poking up, but provided clear fire for us.

I could load and shoot my musket twice in a minute and be accurate in my efforts. If I ply it with more haste, I'll not be so true. The range was fine. The two sides right close in. I brought buck and ball rounds, a killing load to fifty yards. By seventy, the buckshot might not make it lest they had a kindly ricochet or two, and the ball would be doing whatever it damn well felt like.

We had been called to duty during the Battle of Olustee Station in February a year past but ended up assigned to guarding prisoners in Tallahassee, at the Baptist Church and the Masonic Lodge. They were mostly white troops and several blacks, some lightly wounded, others not hurt at all. There were but few negro wounded or taken prisoner to leave out of the field at Olustee. They were shot.

We watched these men for three weeks. We had wanted

in on the fight, and the assignment as jailers sorely disappointed us. I did not profit by it. We were not to speak to them any more than necessary. They were sent on to Andersonville.

Olustee was a grand victory for us but, according to John Wesley, maybe as well we did not make it. The Yankees sent 5,000 troops from Jacksonville, and 2,000 of them ended up casualties. He told me the blood let that day still dwelt in his head.

We had been placed here at a prominent spot on the battlefield, right in the thick of it, most likely, I thought, because we knew what we were doing. We had trained for this. We were disciplined. Good shots. No one had gotten hurt at Newport, and that emboldened us. We also wore matching uniforms. They did not look sharp at the moment. I would put them at disheveled and gamey. But this might have influenced General Miller, being regular Army and all. He had been gray-clad from beginning, his face weather-beat and marked like a road map in witness.

We waited. Then we waited some more. Some of the boys shined their bayonets by sticking them in the sand. Will Rawls had some chaw. The two of us went and stood behind a big pine, and talked and spit.

The reason I'd not met Will before was that he is new in town. His family had moved from Georgia. One of the jobs his father did up there was engraving names and dates on tombstones. He was starting to go on about that, but it was not something I cared to hear about in our present circumstances. I changed the subject.

Is this what they call the lee side of the tree you think? I said.

Lee means out of the wind, Will said. Ain't no wind. Not-in-the-line-a-fire side I'd call this. This is the right side, in other words.

Just then Neil Clary came walking by and saw us and

got in behind the tree with us.

Hey, Virgil, Neil said. Yer buddies said you was o'er this way.

I introduced Neil to Will. They nodded to each other.

That's a nice gun, Will commented.

It is, Neil said, and leaned the weapon backward on his shoulder. Then he stared at Will. There was no malice in the stare, was nothing in it, just an empty thing. I did not know what to make of it.

Right, Will said. Okay, then ... Virgil, I'll see you back at the works. And he left.

After a moment or two I said, What'd you make a Colonel Girardeau?

He's an old sourdough, Neil said. An' whip-smart. He took me in, did not blink.

Neil was looking around.

I'm gone play my wild card at some point. When this thing's on the boil. Get out the back door some way, soon as I find it. Gander around some. I'd like to pick off a couple a them fellers across the way before I do, get in a lick or two. I do not have enough ammo to be in it long. That is the notion I'm workin' on anyway. You did not see me come in, did you?

No, I said.

They makin' fun a yer uniforms o'er there. A bit fancy for 'em. They some good ol' boys, tho'. Say ... that area where Girardeau is set up, behind that cannon by the slough, you ever been through there?

I was in there once in a dry winter, I said. It's some mean bog. An' goes on a bit.

Well, Neil said, I'm thinkin', if I was a clever officer to that side, I'd send me a handful a men, see can they get through there, cross the river and potshot us from behind. An' if it was me, say, I'd detail some raw-bones, maybe some I do not particularly give a shit about—

Or he might would send his best, I said.

That's possible, Neil said. But ... no matter. I have shot

good men before. I can do that.

We soon broke it up, got back to our positions. I did not know it at the time, but that would be our last conversation.

Around 11:00 our pickets withdrew from cover down by the bridge. Captain Butler got our attention and told us calmly: The show is gone flare up shortly. You might hear their canteens and cartridge boxes janglin' when they first get to movin', lest the cannon start, which is a good bet they will. Then you hear nothin' but them. I am told they have three field pieces o'er there.

Load your weapons, he said, cap 'em, full cock. When these goobers come out a the trees, commence to shootin' … an' fire at will.

I soon noticed my breath had gone shallow from listening so hard. And I felt some uncertainty, a little shaky. Hard to allay that. Within five minutes from when the Captain spoke, Yankee cannon opened up on us.

Our guns commenced to speak in reply. And deep-mouthed cannon fire cracked back and forth as the two sides wrangled. Their artillery, for the most part, once again overshot. Shells burst high up and behind us. They whined overhead, haunted metallic voices, a bone to pick. The Yanks sent forth one volley of musketry after another, and some of our troops responded in kind. Then suddenly they burst out full force from the trees around the bridge, and we got to shooting too.

Their blue uniforms and dark skin had blended invisible into the black wood. They flowed out of there now like shadows come to life. Some veered off to the left and some came straight on toward us. They were making a chant sounded like: Hawza, Hawza, Haw … and a number started whooping like they were having just the best time. Then our grape and canister crashed through them.

It is hard to stay collected at first. Hundreds of wild-eyed devils come firing and the high snarl, the sigh of lead looking hard for you can quicken the blood, make you grit your teeth. I bowed my head, I bowed at the waist, let that song spatter into our breastwork or pass on by. There was not a stitch of natural wind that day. But hardware took its stead for a time, and its keening shredded the air.

Bobby Ledsmith put it best.

Right there at first, pshaw! We were properly in the devil's neighborhood, he said.

They had snipers in trees targeting our artillery crews with long distance rifles as the gunners worked their pieces. One marksman in particular was annoying. He'd shot the canteen of a Kilcrease gunner as he was about to take a drink. The ball knocked the canteen out of his hand, now minus several parts, and the tinplate clanged off the gun—he let out a curse, probably at a little higher pitch than he would like to be remembered for—all of which had the crew scrambling. Shot this and that and the other.

The other happened to be a horse. A courier came galloping up looking for General Miller. No one had seen the General of late. Colonel Love? the courier asked. A gunner spoke. Love's way yon, he said, motioned with his hand toward our right flank. And just there the horse fell like its legs had been chopped down. It was a ol' roan farm horse, fond of corn I'd say, came to rest near one of the guns and remained there stone dead so that the crew had to work around it.

Then the sniper hit one of our men as he rammed a powder charge down the barrel on his howitzer. The ball passed through the meat of his leg. I knew him. His family lived not far from mine, name of Putnam. Some of his crew got the blood stanched, and he waited for a litter.

Does it hurt, J.T.? I said.

Not like it ought. I think it would, could I feel it, he said. Smarted some when it bit me, near like a flame. Now it jes' feels asleep … say when you knock yer funny bone?

Gat no pain to it to speak of ...

He said it just so in such a matter-of-fact way.

Now a gunny sergeant with his field-glass located the Yankee sniper by puffs of smoke in an old live oak near a quarter mile distant. The gunny's name was Wendell Beckwith. He'd been to the Mexican war. Wendell was crusty, boundless curses ranting from him. He had mustaches, resembled a big salt-and-pepper bat ornamenting his face. His crew knew what they were doing, and knew to stay clear of him as well—he looked as tho' he might bite. He sighted his gun, loaded with a 12-pound solid shot, and fired it off. The ball went whistling on and, in the best or the luckiest effort of the day, cut the marksman in twain.

There commenced then heavy fighting on our right flank near the river. Things were not behaving there, some disarray. I could see a whole lot better over that way than directly in front of me. The Yanks were crowding the line, about to get the best of it, and our boys started edging back. And shortly the line unraveled.

Now just about near simultaneous to this, the Yankee advance ran upon a sinkhole, which I doubt they knew of till they got to it—easy enough to do there for the smoke and the denseness and tangle. They would be humping through, come to a clear spot and into cold water that got deep on them quick.

They stalled at the sink. Our cannon got hove that way, started to cooking good, and the Yanks pulled back on the double, moved low in the scrub and smoke, and from thence back into timber.

We exchanged a rambling fire for an hour or so. Then it calmed awhile, interspersed with single shots. And finally, quiet settled over the field.

I sat down. I was having some trouble breathing from the smoke. My throat was sore. Taste of black powder. I reviewed a couple things. I was still alive—that was a good sign. I would admire to live a bit longer. I'll not claim to have done well, do not know how I did is the truth of it. When the muskets started rattling in earnest and the cannon to bellow, I could not see worth a damn. I leveled my musket and fired into the smoke and clatter. It had been so windy in Tallahassee, now here the wind was humbled. Smoke wrapped the battlefield and obscured it. The Captain kept telling us to hold under our targets, aim lower. I was not, by any measure, aiming. I loaded and fired flat-out in some version of delirium. If I made any hits, they happened by chance.

You got any water left? I said to Will.

What d'ye say? I can not hear shit, he said, my ears are ringin' so.

The Yankees reformed and shoved at us again. This charge did not go well from the start. Wendell Beckwith bounced a solid shot down the road just as they emerged from timber, and the lead troops went flying about. Right soon behind this, the second Kilcrease gun sent a grape load shrieking to them chest high that acted like a scythe. They did not advance further for the harm brought upon them. They spread out sideways and sniped at us from cover. When the firing slackened after a bit, we could hear the cries of their wounded.

The smoke thinned, and I spotted one of the wounded in the open. I could not see where he was hit, but because of it he had lost his bearings. He was crawling around without destination. I was not the only one noticed him. He was soon peppered and moved no more.

Time unraveled to nothing during the fight. It stopped counting. Was not until things quieted that I noted it moving again and also how poorly I felt. I had slept little, Friday the last good night of that. And since we came on to the field, I'd eaten only a handful of peanuts. My stomach was off. Neil had been right about the cannon. Their muzzle blasts jarred the skull, and they added up on you. I was about to take sick.

I had the notion to wander back behind the artillery, back farther even, past their mules, wanted very much to throw up somewhere alone and collect myself. I for sure did not want to do that in our works. I would never hear the end of it. I'd not have minded if Ma brought me a nice bowl of hot soup either, maybe a slice of bread with mayhaw jelly ... but decided shortly to get all these thoughts out of my head, stay put and back to the business at hand.

Was only a couple minutes later that a long distance minnie ball came amongst us like a damn bumblebee and thumped into Captain Lee Butler's right arm. He was talking to Will and then he yelped, his arm swinging around useless and looked at some odd angle to how it should have been.

I tied it off above the blood slick with my leather string and cinched tight. He chided me. Cussed me good. A litter came. There are normally four litter bearers. Only three showed up. I looked at John Wesley and he said, Go! So I grabbed onto a pole, and we took off.

A minnie ball snarled past the two bearers in front, way too close. One said, Shee-it! and we got to running with our heads tucked down like turtles. Now I could not tell you if it was actually so, but the engagement as a whole seemed to become more spirited just then, the entire battlefield crackling around us. It made for a jolting ride. I saw the Captain's face had a chalky look to it. Then, thankfully, that he had passed out.

We handed him off at a dressing station near the line, a medic there to minister first aid. The medic was young. There was him, a one-mule, two-wheeled ambulance wagon and negro driver, and two nurses. They were set up under a stand of pines. A red flag tied to a low branch marked the location. The medic did his work on a blanket spread on the ground.

Where are my specs? he was saying. Anybody seen my dang ... and presently found them hanging from a little chain around his neck.

He worked on Captain Butler, did not like what he saw. He rubbed morphine into the wound and packed it with lint. The Captain came around, said something or other, but no one could make out any meaning to it. Then he fainted again.

I knew one of the nurses. His name is Henry Wells. I also knew he was not a nurse. Henry is a farrier by trade, has a little shop outside Quincy. He was not involved in treating the Cap, and we spoke.

How did you happen on this duty?

Doc Hentz, he said. I been shoein' his horses for years. When he saw me this morning he said, You gone be a nurse today.

You know anything about it?

Not a tall, Henry said.

The medic wrapped the Captain's arm and made a sling. We loaded him into the ambulance, and it took off to the field hospital.

To the side, in the dark behind a tree, was one of our boys on the ground wrapped in a blanket. It covered his face. Somebody's darlin'.

I asked the medic who it was.

He looked at me blankly.

Sorry, what? he said. I went off some wheres.

Who is that?

John Grubbs, he said. Shot through the heart. You know him?

No.

I did, he said. He told me this morning a plain token come to him that he would be hurt this day.

You gone move him?

He took out his watch, had a look, then snapped it to.

I'll take him home when this day is done, he said. He is

not in any haste now.

I could hear the din behind me, the cannon steady hammering. The Yanks had not stinted on ammunition. They'd brought it all. They were throwing shells at us in their wild manner. Their aim was off—too much big timber in the way, something wrong with their fuses, the powder uneven. Maybe they were just not any good at it. Whatever the reason, they had trouble finding the range of us. Still, and definitely something that began to concern me, the way those boys over that side scattered shot, you knew a good many were strays.

Then I had that qualmish feeling again.

Henry, I said, I got to go o'er behind them gallberries an' throw up.

I know the feelin', he said. I do not believe I'll develop a taste for blood from this day.

Henry wore an old cloth cap. He doffed it a slight bit.

Take care, I said.

You right there, Henry said.

I felt sick now, no bones about it. I wandered back to the gallberry flats, waded in past them to a sandy clearing, and spewed water and smoke. I knelt down on one knee. I wiped my mouth on my coat sleeve. Then over to my right I spotted Neil Clary, up the way there some. He had just come through a tangled cane brake and right soon after got stuck in bramble.

His efforts were comic. He was having a time of it, and watching him I had to grin. It was the first I'd done that seemed for quite a while.

Neil made his way through a thicket of titi, came clear finally, turned and saw me. He stopped in his tracks. When he realized who I was, he hollered my name and held up a pair of boots to show me. He laughed heartily and started my way. Then he disappeared in blood mist and smoke.

A cannon shell had clanged into light directly upon him. I for a split second heard the creaking whistle of its fuse, then saw the flash, felt the sway it caused—just everything got a hitch in it and shrapnel whizzed its angry way. It all took but an instant, a letting out of breath.

Sound took on a tinny-ness. I went to the spot where moments ago Neil stood. There was a burnt area where he had been. And I tell you, powder and hot iron and blood make an awful stank. I came across the twisted barrel of his Henry. Ten feet away I found his right hand and wrist, black and still smoking. There was little else left of him, and I mean that just how it sounds.

I removed his gold band. I put it in a pocket, and threw with all my might what remained of Neil Clary into the brush. I would return the ring to his Ella, I made a promise to him. And I could not help but wonder what he had been up to. How did he get the boots?

I returned to the line. Feeling bad, thoughts of thirst, tiredness, all fell by the wayside. I had just seen a man disappear before my eyes.

There was a break in the fighting.
Will Rawls asked me, How's Cap?
Not so good.
You got blood on your hands, Will said.
I lay on my back looking for a moment or two at my hands and then at the pearl-colored sky, the straw sun.
Your tongue is blue, I told Will.
So's yours, he said.

The Yanks made more attempts from the bridge. We clashed, the fighting raged for a time as they strove to force their way, and we would check them. They'd fall back. A lull would set in. At some point I got the sure sense that what they wanted to happen was just not going to.

During one lull, a roughshod taunting began. Our boys started baiting them. The profane called upon their curses. Those Crackers knew some oaths. There was much ire amongst them. The very thought of Tallahassee being sacked by field-hands got their hackles up. It had happened at Marianna in September of last year, and no one had forgotten.

You heard the place names called out: *Marianna, Olustee, Gainesville ...*

Our officers owned slaves. The rest of us, for the most part, did not. Plantation folks did not let on much difference between Crackers and slaves that I could tell. We were white. That was about it. They would hire overseers from our ranks. Men bearing such names as Maynard or Slaney, Ferrell, Swinehart, Fullwood, chosen for the mean streak in their bones. Otherwise, we were peckerwoods to them.

No quarter the Yanks were being told, tho' in harder terms. They would not be spared. This was no raillery. It was purely mean-spirited. It was venom. Those boys over that way, by caliber, counted no more than but a notch above animal. Tho' a good many of our fighters I suspect thought better of their mule.

The insults directed that way were interrupted now and again by rifles madly barking.

In what turned out to be their last assault, Will commented that they seemed to had lost heart. Will's gun started running hot, until finally he could not remove the ramrod from the barrel.

I might could shoot it out, he said.

You ought not, I said, but just then he fired. The ramrod went sailing.

Lord amighty! I slang that right on out there. I guess we ourt ta check later on, he said, see if any a them boys got speared.

His barrel had split some at the muzzle. He went to borrow a musket from one of the Kilcrease gunners, returned and fired on.

They came at us doggedly that time but no how the same as before. They were following orders now, as soldiers do. They were earning their pay. I think by then we had taken out their best men—the most courageous, the daredevils, and foolhardy. We were posted too well along the line and our crossfire mowed through them, that terrible display of lead and iron. How they withstood it and tried again is beyond reckoning.

I had no love for them whatsoever, and scant pity, but those troops did not lack fight. They had some mettle to them. They were game, but they were being so at right close to point-blank range.

We scotched them good that time. They withdrew, took up positions again in the hammock at the crossing. We could hear their sappers with axes at work across the river, trees felled.

A standoff followed. Sharpshooters on both sides hunted targets. We hunkered down. Hours passed.

Then Lt. Colonel Caraway Smith and his dismounted battalion from the 2nd Florida Cavalry arrived, some 350 veterans. They had come from Lake City by rail to Old Still and marched toward the cannonade. As they approached close on to us they let loose with the yell, that trilling hellcat screech, and entered the field to the sound of fife and drum, carrying a shot-torn white flag with a big red star on it. The color-bearer who held this got into a hard run, and the banner started wagging. A shout rose up along our line. It was the sort of thing you believe war is all about before you knew any better.

The Yanks did not care for it. They drew off over there, back to the bridge, then back to the east side of the river, and firing ceased.

After a time, Colonel Scott sent a line of his horsemen forward. They made their way through the hammock, crossed the bridge to the other side, and found the enemy behind a stout breastwork. Captain Henry Simmons, in command of the skirmishers, got killed there. We found out soon enough that he had charged the works with no regard to his well-being. He was the first to come back across the river, red ribbons in his beard.

Half of Colonel Smith's battalion crossed, and muskets started chattering. I heard it. I was not part of it. A spirited clash sounded like. They were having at it. Then a single cannon came into play over there, and litters started returning to us. We were getting reports from our wounded, but what one said another told differently. They had taken canister loads, that was certain.

The next two wounded that came by us were but lightly hit and Will asked, How's it goin' o'er there? Besides you jes' gettin' your ass shot up an' all.

One said, Middlin'. The other looked at Will like he was some weird thing never before seen in the daylight.

The fight lasted an hour. At that point, their ammunition used up, Smith's men fell back. The Yankees cut bait and started retreating to the coast, did so in such hurry they left dead and wounded behind.

The Battle of Natural Bridge was over.

Our main force crossed the bridge. It was burnt and smoldering. Smell of burnt wet wood. Trees on the bridge were spotted by lead, trees torn and skinned, blood drying on them like paint. Limbs splintered to matchwood. Blue smoke layered high up in the branches and moss. It seemed the only peaceful place and I suspected Old Scratch perched there, surveyed his nether works, made tally of the spoils.

We found negroes scattered here and yon and whithersoever. We came across the slain and some still writhing. Across remains charred, stench of burnt hair. Across men that had bled out. I noticed off to the north along the riverbank, just to the side of a big cypress stump, a flash of blue—a bit of color that was there and just as quickly gone. It could have been a jay flitting was my first thought, but then again, I doubted there was any bird or wild critter at all left to come nigh this broken place.

I went over that way and soon felt uneasy. I felt it keenly. I edged around the stump, cocked and leveled. There was a sergeant setting with his back against the cypress. His left leg, that closest to me, had been blown off just below the knee. There was no blood. Whatever took his leg, the heat of it cauterized the wound. He was a big buck, jet black, broad-chested. I had him covered but began to think there was no need of it. He looked ahead, a blank expression, his mouth slack, not sure even how aware he was of me. He shuddered once. Then, with his right hand, raised a pistol to his ear, cocked it and fired.

Some of my buddies came running.

Hey, look, Charlie said. Virgil kilt un.

No, I said. He done it his own self.

I picked up the pistol. A Colt Navy revolver. 1851 model. I checked the chamber. He had saved the last shot for himself. I put the pistol in my tote and have it still. The ball sent him to Heaven or left him obliged to the devil, only he could say. It made a mess of his head and is not something I wish to dwell on, ever.

Now nobody asked, and I did not volunteer the information, but because of the direction I approached him, I had not seen that pistol till he raised it.

We went on, across ground cumbered by dead and wounded, and reached the first Yankee breastwork, cut trees and stumps ricked up and shoveled dirt, where we found negroes stacked together, their bodies riddled. They tried to bury some in the breastwork, done in haste, had not made a good job of it. I saw blood and bone covered in dirt, the human body broken into parts and scraps as in the devil's winepress.

We found one soldier impaled by a horseshoe. It stuck in his chest. Artillery is a brutal craft. You never knew how our gunners might contrive their grape loads. I had noticed the Kilcrease boys loading big fishing line sinkers and links of chain. There was another trooper I saw no wound on and was curious if he had been scared to death. Then I noticed just the smallest ragged cut on his forehead where shrapnel had ripped into him. His eyes were wide open. He looked quite surprised this had happened.

Then a second breastwork, made of felled pines with their tops pointed toward the crossing, and more of the same tho' in lesser numbers. I saw a dead trooper there, on his back, his right arm locked outstretched to the sky, looking for a hand up from the Lord I took it.

The area was strewn with cartridge boxes, mess kits, greasy haversacks. We found hardtack. They had a reddish color, three-inch square, near a half-inch thick. We knew what they were but could not figure out how to eat one without breaking a tooth. We skipped them like flat stones across the water of a little pond off to the left of the works.

Bobby Ledsmith found a bayonet and, soon after, a tobacco bag. That was a popular item. We came across pages torn from a Bible. I picked one up, a page from Malachi, that I folded and put in my pocket.

I was busy cutting brass buttons off a Yankee coat when Del Olney gave a shout. He had come upon a white soldier, a round through his neck. Del was shook.

He stared at me, Del said. I turned 'im over, and he stared right at me with them dead eyes.

I looked at the man's eyes. They did not seem aimed at anything in particular.

John Wesley ambled over our way to see what we found so of interest. The man had been stripped down to his long underwear, and not by any of us. There were more Bible pages scattered about him.

I'll be sworn, John Wesley said, taking in the scene. What the hell was they doin' o'er here?

He an officer? I asked.

He is for sure white, John Wesley said. We need to bury this un. No cypress for the dead today. Bury him face down.

And we did so.

The cadets suffered only one fatality, Tommy Frazier, who fell from a rail car. Death snatched him away and laid him down to rest. Barney Cliett had his bayonet snapped in two by ball or shrapnel, he did not know which. The force of it knocked him flat. His head snapped back when he hit the ground and cracked a tooth. One of the Tucker brothers had a bullet scar on his rifle stock. Leffie Conklin suffered a black eye and the right side of his face swollen. His musket had bucked on him. He thought he might have loaded it twice before he fired. Jim Euler had a ball go through his cartridge box. Cade Lawrie fell apart for a time, but not until it was all over. He did well as any of us during the fight, maybe better, as he is a dead shot. Afterwards he started crying. Then he got to laughing sort of crazy. And went back and forth like that atween the two. It took him a good while to settle down. No one said anything about it, not then nor later that I know of. He worked out aloud what a good many of us felt like inside.

No wounded.

Here is what I recall now when I think about that day: Tommy gone so young. I know that he had yet to love a girl, might not have even kissed one. And a man I thought well of, blown away like he were no more than thistle seed. Or how a minnie ball when it hits bone, the bone shatters like glass. The coppery smell of blood and how bright red its color. And how the air real often had sharp edges, that cut from far away.

I made it through untouched as do all who are untouched in battle, by God's grace, and luck.

I walked that field in my thoughts many times long afterwards, nobody else anywhere near. The wounded still call out there. And the dead have not diminished their concern. No cure has come to them.

In the following days I would take out that page from the Bible I found, the first chapter of Malachi, and go to one passage: *And I hated Esau, and laid his mountains and his heritage waste for the dragons of the wilderness.*

The enemy wounded were attended to. Those still breathing but torn up bad got put out of their misery by bayonet. The dead were thrown into sinkholes. A rumor spread that two Yankee scouts had been found shot that somehow made their way across the river up above us. No one seemed to know how it happened or who killed them. I wanted to ask, Did one not have his boots no more?

Since then, I have seen casualties from gun fight, razor, and fire, but at the time it was my first experience with violent human death. I saw that the body remained in varying degrees of holes and rents, but that the main ingredient had moved away. The dead are not there anymore, is what I saw, and that the body alone is but a paltry affair and no more than a house abandoned.

Time was spent clearing the river road of felled trees so our cavalry could tail the Yanks toward the coast and make sure of their intentions. They had obstructed the road well on their way out. Colonel Scott rode with what looked to be a half company of men, those most familiar with the countryside I would think, but then again they might have been the only ones left whose mounts were not jaded.

The battle done, a quiet settled amongst us. Smell of powder residue in the air.

At sunset, a solitary yell rang out. A thousand voices joined in. A few men fired their weapons into the air. Most had enough shooting for the day.

And after a while, before anyone was ready for it surely, a bugle sounded assembly. We fell in, gathered up in marching order and started moving. We marched in pitch dark down the east side of the river this time, a wild road, no more than a wallow, and knotted with cypress knees. The Yanks had been up and down it, and now we followed in the muck, stumbling along like drunkards. Word came back finally, around one in the morning, told of how the Yanks had crossed the East River Bridge down by the coast, burned it and were headed to their ships.

The past hour or so I had marched while dreaming. I felt like no more than a pack mule. We were somewhere close on to Newport.

We bivouacked by the river under rustling pines. Some of the boys built a bonfire with old split rail fencing they found nearby. In the light of the fire we looked at one another, faces black with powder. We spoke in hoarse voices, red-eyed, shoulder sore. We stank.

John Milton's body-servant showed up, fixed a pole resting on crotched sapling stakes, and put on a mess-kettle of beans to cook. I was surely hungry but did not get to those beans until morning. I had a hard enough time taking my shoes off, my feet blistered and swole up so. I recall listening to an owl down along the river. I thought of Neil Clary. I said aloud to him, Helluva day, buddy.

And that is all I remember of it.

We lay up in place until it was known for sure the Yankee ships had departed and did not get back to Tallahassee until the evening of the 9th. On the roofs of boxcars we rode into town, where pretty girls placed wreaths of laurel and wild olive on our caps, and spoke of us as heroes.

1868

Along the Manatee River
Late March

The leaves have come out on the live oaks all at once.

I gathered my gear and said goodbye to the Lambs. Or more rightly to the son Dool, who was the only one up and about just then. I wandered down to the wharf, spoke to an old man fishing about where I might hire a horse, that I wanted to get to Snead Island. He directed me to Hawley's Livery. Mr. Hawley, he said, ships in mustangs from Texas time to time. I can not vow they got any jes' now. If not, he'll rent you a old mule. He is blind, he added.

Mr. Hawley?

No, the mule, he said.

Town was a sandy lane through the hammock, a few buildings here and there made of pine weathered grey, an ox yoked to a two-wheeled cart tied to a post. The beast chewed cud, barely awake.

It is the third spring since Natural Bridge. After the battle the cadets went back to doing what we had been doing, which did not seem like much after our experience. We were full of ourselves. We were slightly intoxicated by it all. I held to the thought that my life before then had been no more than a child lost in play.

Then the reckoning came.

On April 1st, Governor Milton, at his Jackson County estate, died in a shotgun accident as he was about to go bird hunting. General Lee surrendered on the 9th at Appomattox Courthouse, Virginia. It took a week for that news to reach Tallahassee, brought with it a sense of the heart riven. Shops closed except for those selling spirits. Women went to their parlors to be with children and friends. Hard men gave way momentarily on the street, then composed themselves, walked on. On the 11th, Lincoln was assassinated. There was an indifference in town, at best, to the shooting of the president, tho' it did not seem to me that it helped in any way. It just kept things crazy. On the 26th of the month, General Joe Johnston surrendered the last army of the South at Greensboro, N.C. The day after I heard that news, I packed up and headed home.

There is a circular drive around the seminary that joined the Quincy road to the west. It ran into the hammocks out of town. It is a cotton road along which six-mule-team wagons had hauled bales for decades, and carved walls into the red clay along the sides. Mockingbirds sang to me all the way home.

I learned from friends that midway through May the school closed, that bluecoats had taken possession of the town. The seminary buildings became Yankee barracks. I heard that negroes from the plantations in the area soon filled the roads into Tallahassee, then the streets of the town itself, all wanting a glimpse of the troops that meant their freedom.

At home I held tight to what I had and added up what was gone. It is hard to go on as if nothing is altered when you have lost your country—that dream come to naught and now extinct, that brought so many heroes to their tomb and vacant chairs at kitchen tables. I had varied thoughts on the War. I hated that we lost. But I was not humbled by it nor went about long-faced. That storm had passed, and I was thankful.

We had not heard from Pa for a good long while, and it kept on into the summer of that year, no word, nothing. I'd sit on the porch and watch for his wagon and team to turn up the lane to our house. I tried to will it to happen, but my will was not strong enough, my hopes in vain. He did not come home.

Three springs and I could not tell you exactly what I had been up to. Time went by. Some of it time misspent. I let my hair grow long. I learned how to drink. I got into immoderation for a while. It did not fit me well, but I kept at it some.

I placed Neil Clary's ring in my Bible, and it set there waiting. I got in the practice of speaking to him. I kept him in mind.

I worked our farm. I worked hard. When my thoughts strayed from work to larger affairs, I never felt certain about anything.

Pa did not leave us poor. He'd made a habit of exchanging dollars for gold, as he never trusted Confederate paper. Ma told me his last exchange had been fifteen thousand graybacks for 250 in gold coin. Not so long after that, the currency became worthless. The pinch came and the pinch stayed. It costs a sight of money to live these days, but we will make it through.

I found Hawley's livery, the doors wide open, a very dark negro in a leather apron named Sam working there, repainting the establishment's sign in gray and yellow. There were three small corrals behind the shop, log pens. Hawley was not around, gone to Key West for something or other Sam told me. Be back, Sam said, when he git back.

I accepted the mule, as there was no other animal on the premises. It was an old jack mule, lean and lank, pale red in color, with a white muzzle and milky eyes. Sam fixed a rope around his neck and nose that served as a halter. No blanket, no saddle.

Ye know mules?

Sure.

Ye dismount, hold dat rope tight. Or he gone run off.

Got it.

He grow up out dere, Sam said, know his way an' back. Ye'll come to a cut. Might could wade tru. Depend on de tide. He'll not. He doan like crossin' water. Zif he afraid hit gone play a trick on 'im. Take de halter off. Leave hit. Thout dat, he gone find sometin' to eat. Den he head back. He not zactly blind …

He thought for a moment.

Might do some fartin', he added.

The mule had an easy gait. We followed the river west, walked the white shore line, dense live oak hammock inland. Blue jays raising cane. Redfish tailing in low water and mullet jumping. Once, as we passed a spot, a gust of wind troubled the surface—then it boiled and exploded from a bait school struck from below. Terns and gulls appeared from nowhere, wheeled down for scraps.

After a while we came upon a rowboat and shortly to a spare-made older gent with a long gray beard who was dowsing for water.

Virgil, I said.

Scully.

You from here abouts?

Tampa, he said. Me and the wife visitin' the McNeils. They by the pond there in town. My wife's a cousin.

I noticed one of his eyes was blue, the other brown.

I got down from the mule, tethered him, and spoke with Scully awhile. He explained to me which different woods were best for dowsing, green sapling gum being his favorite, willow a close second. He took out a flask and offered me a drink. It felt light, he had been at it. The whiskey had a smoothness to it, unusual for these parts. Mostly what you got was rough cob. He told me where I could purchase some, from a man who owned a general store across the river at Palma Sola. Name of Otis Pike.

He could sell shit to a stable, so make sure you get what

you paid for, Scully said. Then he took the flask and wiped the rim, held it up. Better times, he said, and finished it off.

Step back a pace, Scully said. That damn mule is too close.

I stepped back.

He will kick you for his own amusement, he said. Where you headed?

The Mayfield place.

That would be on a ways, he said. Keep to the shoreline best you can.

He looked me over, the knapsack I carried, blanket roll strapped on top.

You do not look like a drummer, he said.

No, I said. My Pa was. But ... not me. I have not a thing to sell.

You the second feller I seen out here today. The Haden kid is around. He is about a giant, tho' only a boy. You run across him, do not let his size put you off. He is gentle. Louis is his first name I believe. Boy is crazy about plants. He stands in one place too long, he bound to take root. It is good to see young folks around agin, he said.

We talked some more, then said our goodbyes. Listening to him, I got the sense that he was not so interested in whether he found water with his dowser wood. He was out here to get away from his wife and do some drinking in peace.

I came across the kid down by the cut. I let the mule loose. He started dining on young blackjack leaves. Once off the mule, I felt like I was walking a bit sideways for some reason, a little sashay to the right. It let me in on that maybe the fever was coming back. It started up the evening past. I felt better when I woke. I had really hoped it was but the overnight variety.

Name is Lou, he said.

I am six feet tall. We were near eye to eye. And he was a whole lot wider than me. He wore a green straw hat, looked about half finished, plaited out of palmetto as he walked about. He showed me some red-stem-and-leaf plants.

They roselle, he said. They bloom around Thanksgivin', an' it is special to see, a soft, dark-red color. Mostly you find 'em where a house used to be. Folks lived here once I'd think.

He was picking seed pods as he spoke.

They called Florida cranberry, tho' I have never tasted a cranberry, so ... I do not know if there is any sameness to them. His face wrinkled into a grin. Makes good tea, he said.

He touched some leaves on a small tree. This is buttonwood. Touched another. They guava. I see these growin' all over now. Ma makes jelly from their fruit. That there is a coco plum ...

I saw that he could carry on awhile in this vein.

I'm lookin' for the Mayfield place, I said.

I was jes' there, he said. I'll take you. He pointed to his boat, an old skiff with a new sail. We'll be there in no time. This cut, he said, a gale come through here in olden days, carved Snead into an island.

We got situated in the boat. Bundle up, he said. He let the sail out, the sail bent to the wind, and we started flying. I had noted the fever, but the boat ride cooled it down. We passed flamingo feeding in the flats, 10-15 of them, the first I ever saw. He showed me olive branch cuttings he took from the Mayfield midden. An old tree, he said. Likely an olive pit grown up from when the Spanish first came here. I have not seen it make any olives. Not sure why that is—

He pointed to the middle of the river. I looked that way. In a moment or two, a big long fish jumped. It must have been nine foot.

Sturgeon, I said.

Yep. They's bigerns in here than that.

Turned out he lived further south. So he had to get along home. He dropped me off. I said goodbye, walked past a rowboat upturned on shore, and took the path to the house on the shell midden. There is a long wide field below the mound. A seine net hung from a tree limb, a small scaffold nearby for drying fish. Smell of orange blossoms, tho' slight. The grove was young, six, seven years old seemed like, and not producing all out yet. A big kitchen garden, corn sprouts poking up in part of it. Ripe tomatoes. Off to the left of the walking path, a negro woman hoed around an orange tree. She had a ginger-cake color to her, wide hips, high cheekbones. She wore a dress of simple homespun and blue head rag. There were maybe two hundred young orange trees in this area, and bananas and Indian pumpkin along both sides of the field.

I nodded to her. She studied me a moment, then went on with her hoeing. I put her down as a crazy sort who lived in her head which, as it turned out, was not exactly the case, but close. Now, once again, I felt the grippe gaining on me. It was more than a notion. My body ached. A light brown fice came a-hollering. The negro woman said, Hush, dawg! and it turned around smartly and found something better to do.

I walked up the steep path to the house. I'd had misgivings about this visit for years. Now all those misgivings rekindled. Miss Mayfield was sitting on a bench in the sun mending a shirt. She wore an ankle length and long sleeved blue cotton dress, many times washed, buttoned at the neck, barefoot. We greeted one another. I put my tote down, removed my hat and introduced myself. I felt odd. My body inhospitable. I said, I been stayin' at rough lodgings. It was something I had in my mind but had not thought to say aloud, and it surprised me that I did so.

I thought you were someone else for a moment, she said.

Ma'am, I have ...

I said that, reached down for my tote and, as I was told later, blacked out.

There is a narrow porch along the front of the house. I came to and found myself on it propped in a rocking chair, the women wrapping my blanket around me. I woke again on a pallet bed sometime later.

Miss Mayfield stood nearby wearing a long brown sweater over her dress, and the negro woman sat on a hide-bottomed chair beside the bed. We were not in the main house but at a palmetto hut nearby, tho' at the time I did not know where the hell I was, nor cared. A smudge fire was burning outside. This to discourage spirits, not mosquitoes, too cold for them just then. It is but another thing I found out later on.

This is Sugarbee, Miss Mayfield said. She'll watch over you.

I woke later, the day fading in the doorway, dim light from a smoky candle. I had a wool blanket covering me, my own blanket underneath it, my coat … I was still cold. My teeth were clattering. I felt like I was about to shake apart. Sugarbee sat away from the candle, a dark form, quiet. She left and later returned with a deer hide, added it to my covers. I slept. I dreamed of swimming in a bed. Then it was dawn. I awoke to it everything about me soaked.

Sugarbee brought clean clothes, a dry blanket. She stepped outside, and I changed. The clothes she brought were big on me. She returned with a bucket of water, dipper in it, a bowl of coffee. She had a high forehead, hawk nose, something fierce in her bearing. I was thirsty. I drank. I fell asleep again. When I woke, Sugarbee was sitting on a mat on the floor beside the bed.

Look, you, she said. You be in yo right mind?

Well, I said, I think so. Close on to it anyways.

She picked up my tote. She had taken everything out of it already, now she started putting it all back—tin mug, knife and spoon, match box, my razor and stone, money, my Colt revolver—

That is loaded, I said.

Woyk best dat way, she said.

She put the pistol in my tote, ammo. My Bible was the only item left.

She removed Neil's ring from the pages of the Book.

I knows who dis belong to, she said. I known he gone, a long time now. I know hit sure. But her doan. An' I tell you, to see dis ... gone break her heart. 'T will bound her to sorrow, an' I'll not allow such. Her still believe Neil come back.

She looked away. She had slow eyes. They were slow to attach onto their object, even slower to separate from it.

Where he keeled?

Near Tallahassee, I said.

He on his way home den.

Yes.

Tings stacked against her, she said, been most a year now. I's 'fraid her gone tip o'er. She turned to me again. I put hit 'pon you, she said. Keep dis ...

She placed the ring in the Bible and back in my tote, closed it up.

She gave me a spoonful of nostrum that said on the bottle: Mrs. Winslow's Soothing Syrup. She left the hut. The medicine knocked me out. I remember little of that day or night, but for waking now and again very thirsty, drinking water, sleep ...

Grumbling sky, a cranky dawn, fishy breeze off the river. Sugarbee cleaned me up, gave me dry clothes once more. I asked her who they belonged to. My son, she said. She had two children she told me, Tissy and Loyal. Tissy was still around. She had taken up with a man in Oak Hill, not far away up river, and inland some. Loyal had disappeared toward the end of the War. She thought sure he headed to Jacksonville, Federal held at the time, and to the North eventually. He wanted to meet the President. He was curious to see snow. And then to make ice cream from the

snow, as someone told him that is how they did.
Be a fool boy, she said.

Rain came drizzling down the rest of that day and on into the next. I did not see much of either woman. They worked in the rain. They checked on me, brought food and water, administered more nostrum, which I came to like. Sugarbee switched it up several times. Once with quinine. Then with whiskey and pepper. That one did not suit me.

They were tired from work and offered little conversation. No matter. A couple times as they spoke to me, the candle flickering and shadows dancing about, I could not keep my eyes open. I awoke after a while, and they'd be gone. Even awake, I did not feel exactly in the world. I had stepped outside.

The hut was small, 12 foot by 14 maybe, built of palm fronds, dirt floor half-covered with woven mats, the pallet bed made of log and board and not far off the ground, the bed tick filled with pine needles and moss, my pillow a corn sack. Hanging off to the side, a muslin mosquito bar full of holes. A turkey-wing fan, from a down and out turkey by the looks of it. The ceiling not much taller than me. Slop jar. The door was a makeshift affair that sagged on its wooden hinges, did not particularly want to close. The wind stepped in as it liked. Two windows made of driftwood propped open by sticks. Outside there was that mangrove-wood smudge fire, put sand on it to smoke.

I awoke again. Three guinea hens stopped by to check on me, looked in the doorway awhile, discussed the situation amongst themselves, then sped away, and the wind blew hard on a bright cold morning. I had made it through the fever. That day I was on my feet again, tho' moving around in a half stumbling manner, as if I'd forgotten how to get about. By my reckoning, it was April 1st.

I walked the midden. It wandered like ridges throughout the property, parallel to the river, the house on the highest part, and that part level. There was a step down off to the west and an apron there, a slightly smaller, flat area than that where the house stood. It was level and circular, and served as their kitchen.

I found the shitter, a quarter moon carved on the door. No star. There was a palmetto patch behind the hut for to do my business. I came across Sugarbee's shanty on a small mound close to the river, a rough plank structure with a front door on one side and a window with shutters on the other. I soon learned that she closed these of a night no matter the weather to rebuke the hants. I stuck my head in the window and had a look. A pallet, her clothes hung from wall pegs. She slept here, looked like, and little else. On the path to the shanty and on the one that led away from it, small-animal skulls and bird skulls hung like ornaments in the bushes.

Otherwise, I just enjoyed the morning, the sun splintering down through the woods, and that I was out walking again.

That afternoon while Sugarbee worked in the field, I spoke to Miss Mayfield. It was my first time alone with her. Sugarbee had been present before, eyes like nail heads, wary sideways glance. I had a secret to keep. She wanted to make sure I kept it.

There was a plank table next to the outdoor kitchen, benches alongside, a pail of water and a gourd dipper on it. We sat there. The kitchen was located on the apron I spoke of, 15 feet from the house, and consisted of two fire circles made of limestone rock and conch shell. Pots hung from fire-irons. It is where Sugarbee cooked unless the rains prevented. I would learn in time that the rain had to fall like to pin her to the ground before she would move to the hearth inside.

You gave us a scare, Miss Mayfield said. Thought you

might break a bone, shakin' like you was.

I appreciate you carin' for me, I said. I am beholdin'. It was an odd case of grippe. Jes' the fever, an' not much else you would expect of such.

Sug was all-fired sure, she said, you'd come down with Yella Jack. I thought not. This is hardly the time of year for it, tho' ... who knows. Jack could be changing things up.

I had it when I was a kid. A mild case, my parents said, whenever they spoke of it. I was only three. I have no memory on it. But ... I'll not get it again. I'm immune. Sugarbee not afraid?

It is common opinion, in New Orleans anyway, that negroes do not take sick with it same as we do. Not sure why that would be. Or even if it's true. But, no ... Sug is not afraid of much.

A doctor once told me red-heads catch it less so'n most folks, I said.

Right there is the problem, she said. They know little more than we do.

Well ... he laughed when he said it. Ole Doc Bigbie. He has a practice over to Quincy, close to where our farm is. We had a conversation about the fever one time, settin' on a bench out front of the courthouse. Tho' ... conversation is not the best word. I listened. I was shakin' my head up and down quite a lot. Seemed like that was my part in it.

Doc is well known to errant citizens—he would treat gonorrhea for five dollars, whereas others in the area might take thirty from you. This is not something I mentioned to Miss Mayfield.

He liked to test his own medicines time to time, I said, see if they worked like they ought to. It made him talkative. On a normal day, he'd just mumble if you spoke to him. He has an easy-going but diverted manner. Might grab your wrist out on the street as you spoke to him an' take your pulse, tell you, You'll be fine, and walk away. Not sure how we got onto yellow fever. It came up somehow or other. An' he commenced to tell me the various treatments modern doctors render, to see if they can get a handle on it. Sounded like torture …

All these words amounted to a near outburst on my part, more than I had spoken for days on end, and after it I sat there a bit off kilter.

She put her face toward the sun, took in the light.

We should have cool nights, warm afternoons for a while now, she said. When you get well enough, maybe you can explain to me what in the world you doin' here. You nigh have to be lost to fetch up here.

How you know what the weather will be? I said.

I can foretell it, she said.

How about hurricanes?

No big storms this year, she said.

We'll have to see about that, I said.

The old people talk about the gale of '48 that emptied the river for a time. It sucked all the water out to the Gulf.

That was a storm, I said.

F'true. They say a doe wandered the riverbed. There will not be a storm like it this year. That is my prediction. She smiled a little at this.

Big April wind all that next day, chop on the river. I was sitting on the porch with Miss Mayfield at noon. The house is elevated on wedge-shaped piers of heart cypress. A steep pitched roof of cedar shakes. It was not so long ago built. The wood had drawn together nicely, the house sound and tight.

We were eating bananas and having coffee. She was crazy about coffee it seemed. It had been in short supply during the War, short meaning there was none.

We made cornbread coffee for awhile, she said. That is just wrong. It is not civilized. We finally settled on okra seed. Dried and parched, it made the best substitute. I still use elderberry ink to write. We had no oil for our lamps, either, she said. Still do not, too expensive far as I'm concerned. Cold spells, I read by the fireplace. And we have decent candles now. During the War, our homemades never did burn right. They smoked terrible.

I found Sugarbee's shanty the other day when I was walkin' around, I said.

Not much to it, Miss Mayfield said, but she likes that she has her own place. I'm surprised you made it there and back in one piece. She claims that path is guarded by spells.

Guarded by possum heads, more like it, I said.

This property belongs to my cousin, Lee, she said. Lee and his wife, Emma. I am taking care of it. I hope to buy it someday, if things work out that way. They are down in Sarasota now, on a midden there her family owns. They had a child last year, a little girl named Katie. Emma is a sweet soul, but she is not hardy. She needed help with the baby. Nor, I think, did she like being away from her kin so long. That family is close-knit … she missed them.

The Mayfields are from New Orleans originally, she went on. She pronounced it N'Awlins.

Back in '59, the Northern Lights made their way to the city. Did you see them here? Near the end of August that year? I heard they went way on down to Cuba.

I did, I said. My little brother was not more'n a baby then. I was holdin' him in my arms. He kept reachin' a hand up, tryin' to touch 'em or grab on.

We lived down in the Garden District, she said. We were on the verandah, a Sunday evening … half past eight and sultry as could be. It is one of those times you recall so distinctly. Aunt Adele sat next to me fanning herself. I looked at her, then past her to the night sky. It had turned blood red and started dancin'. I thought it the prettiest thing I'd ever seen. I took it for the Lord's signature.

Daddy fancies himself an astronomer, she said, tho' an amateur one to be sure. He knows the constellations. He found the stars good company. He always referred to the night sky as the *Element*, as if it were all one thing—one thing with many facets, like a diamond, say. He sought counsel from the *Element*—believed that a good augury might come to you, or a bad. I never understood quite what he meant by all that. How it worked, or even rightly if it did. He is known to make something up to see if he can get it over on me.

But whereas I thought the lights were the All Mighty scribbling His name, to Daddy they foretold a change of fortune. He saw bad tidings headed our way, and they were just around the corner.

He knew the War was coming, I guess anyone who paid attention did by then. Knew the city would be a target early on. Lincoln would want our cotton, the port and the river. Over the next year or so Daddy got to doing what was necessary for us to leave if it came to that. He liquidated some holdings ... land, business partnerships. The cooper shop was his main business. It was important to New Orleans, to the sugar trade. My grandfather three times back started it. It was a big operation by the time Daddy took over. He set up two of my cousins to run it. And he started looking into for a place we could escape to.

He was convinced the Yankees would get beyond bearing. He did not want me scarred by it. Mama was gone by then, been so awhile. I am their only child.

Then in '62 all that he foresaw was put in motion, and we had not yet gotten out. The city fell in April. As a present to the Yankees, folks set about spoiling all the sugar in the parish. Burnt the steamships at the wharves. The planters dumped their cotton in the river or torched it. The bales did not all catch like you would think. A good many of them smoldered, smell of burning clothes.

After that, they wanted us to take the oath of allegiance. Many did, became fake Yankees and laughed it off, but

Daddy had no intention of doing so, nor living with such people.

The War Comet showed up in early summer, another sign from the *Element*. The comet came and stayed on, night after night … that bright token. When I think on it now, I see that comet was an outrider for the old life.

Finally, we quit our home and came here. Daddy knew Major Gamble since back in the '40s. He had a big plantation up river, she said, past the village. 3500 acres.

Daddy's cooperage made sugar barrels. Major Gamble ordered a number of thousand pound barrels and had them shipped. Daddy came along to guarantee delivery.

He'd always had a curiosity about Florida. And he liked to travel. He and PaPa went to London one time. They were there on business, but they had some fun, too. They found the city way too big and gone to rack. One thing dawned on them right quick—there were no negroes in London. This was shocking to them. PaPa discovered Scotch whiskey over there. He did not drink all the time, but when he got started he went full tilt at it. The Scotch got him started. He had a severe drawl, which magnified when he drank. When he talked to people there, Daddy said, the accents were so thick on both sides of the conversation, neither understood much of what was being said. Whenever that trip was spoken of tho' … no negroes in London is what they always came back around to. They never got over that ...

I had the Gamble brothers on my mind as she spoke, John and Robert. They are from Tallahassee and familiar to me. I did not think much of them, but held my tongue, thankfully.

Whenever Major Gamble came to New Orleans, he and Daddy got together and painted the town, she said. They never got home before dawn. Daddy was always game for a night out.

I remember the Major from when I was but little. I thought him handsome. He was my idea of a gentleman.

He sold his plantation before the War. In '56 or '7. Got into debt, sugar prices fell, the Indian war ... I think he even owed Daddy money. But he still had a little property over in Oak Hill that needed tending and was glad to have us there. His plantation did not fare well. The Yankees raided it in '64 and ruined the sugar mill.

It was sad leaving New Orleans, she said. Our family's been there forever. We might not have exactly left our mark, but we were there.

Goodness, she said. I am ever so sorry. I can not seem to stop talkin'.

No need to apologize, I said.

I liked hearing her accent to tell the truth, something very pleasant to it. It was charming—not a word I use often, but the right one. From time to time I got so caught up in the music of it, I would lose track of what she was saying.

Neil had told me: She is easy to be around.

How did you get out?

Of the city? At night. She grinned. By boat. It took some doin'. Daddy bribed somebody or other I imagine.

Lee left the city soon after we did, she went on, and enlisted at Shreveport. He served with the Orleans Light Horse, a cavalry outfit. He fought at Stones River and Chickamauga. He was a prisoner of war near Rome, Georgia, when the War ended.

I doubt he cared for that, I said.

He ate salt mule. Did not say much else on it. It was not something he wished to recall. He was freed that summer. They gave him five days provisions for his return to New Orleans. He went there and sold his home and land, and came here. He bought this 40 acres and started on the house. Lee is a good carpenter. He can do most anything with wood.

It's a fine house, I said.

The house had about it a cabinet-maker's precision, a craftsman had been at work.

When he started, nails were hard to come by, she said. He found some finally and used them on the flooring and roof. The rest of the house is put together by mortise and tenon joints, and wooden pegs. The trusses and joists are heart pine. It will be here awhile I think.

Soon on he met Emma. Everything just came together for him, and did so in a hurry. Seemed like he belonged to be here. Now Daddy is back to New Orleans. He's hardly the frontier sort, tho' he made do. He missed the city dearly.

You goin' back?

Maybe. Some day. Daddy wants me to. But I'll tell you, this place has a root-hold sense to it. You stay awhile, it takes you in.

Daddy says they have an ice factory in the city now, she said. They manufacture ice some way. How nice would that be? Have some orange juice with sugar and ice on a summer's day?

She had a straw hat held loosely by a ribbon at the back of her neck.

What come of his cooper shop? I said.

The Yankees took it over. He has filed a reparations claim, but ... Had as well forget that I think.

She stood and looked around some, then picked up an old cedar bucket to show me. It was a three-gallon bucket, a hemp-rope bale. This is what they started making, way back at the beginning of the business, she said. They used cattail roots for caulking. Over time, about everyone in New Orleans had one of these.

Some green parrots flew by, high up, quick. Mostly I heard them, that ratchety, chain-clank song of theirs, if parrots can be said to have a song. It reminded me.

I heard a horn this morning, I said.

That dulcet tune? She smiled. That was Sug blowing her conch shell, calling down the guineas. They roost in the trees around her place. Or sometimes she might just want to wake the light. Not to say she needs an excuse to do whatever she is minded to.

I got to talking about my family's farm, located halfway between Tallahassee and Quincy.

About the time I was born, I said, Pa started planting pecans. Now we have a orchard, 30 acres or so. Early on he planted because he liked to eat pecans. Then he kept on at it.

Nice to walk the orchard now, to see how he had dreamed it. 'T was for his olden years. But he is gone. Pecans the only thing makes money for us. Long time ago he raised tobacco. It was the kind a tobacco leaf used to wrap cigars. That was too much work, and he quit it.

The rest of our farmin' is jes' for us to eat. Hogs and corn and beans ... chickens. Ma got some hatching eggs once, what turned out to be Dominickers. She took a fancy to the breed, and that is all we have now. Some wild-ass scrub cattle, ol' mossyhorns. You want anything a them, you need take along a gun. Two sorrel mules. Mules is all we ever had. I have yet to own a horse. Ma, long as I remember, kept a big kitchen garden. She still dabbles in it some, but my sis has taken on the hard work.

Sis is a old maid. She got interested in rum the last couple years. Might be a problem ... I shrugged. She'll never find a man. She is gone too inward. Bein' married to her might be a whole lot like livin' alone. She hardly talks anymore.

Sug does not have that problem, Miss Mayfield said.
I noticed.

We get on well enough, tho' at times it takes some effort on my part. Daddy was given three slaves when he came of age. Sug's mama, Lottie, was one of them. Lottie was young then, 13 or so. Me and Sug most likely have common blood.

I looked away. I did not want to get into that. My family

had never owned slaves. We could not afford them.

Sugarbee told me about her children, I said.

How many she speak of?

Two.

She had another, a girl, Jerusalem. She was her youngest. A bull shark took her, upriver, near the village.

We sat quiet a moment.

Who's the father? I said.

Different one for each. She is just all nig sometimes.

Jerusalem's father was a mustee, she said. As white lookin' as you or me. He was freeborn. Boy had green eyes. He only spoke French, and she … whatever that is she talks. Women noticed him. He'd tomcat around and get crossways with her. When she got wind he was two-timin' her, they brawled. She fought him like a man. Daddy finally gave him some money and told him to get lost 'fore she kilt him.

She looked at me. Your farm …

Not much to do there right now. We prune in the winter. We done fertilized already. What y'uns fertilize with?

We compost seaweed and mullet, she said, oak leaves. Takes some time, but it works good. The piles are down by the water. Far enough away so as not to smell them while they curin'.

The mullet are so thick at times you have to wade through them, she said. They make a run up river at night, you can barely sleep for the racket.

Last year we started thinnin', I said, takin' out ev'ry other tree, as they have grown into one another bad. The way we do things, the job will last a while. My brother is probably there this very minute, lookin' for to shoot a crow or squirrel, or maybe a bunch a mistletoe.

In summer, caterpillars make nests. We have to get into the trees with a torch. I leave that job to my brother. I get up five feet above ground, I am in danger. I like to fall. I mean, I do not much like it, but I've made it a habit.

My brother is still a kid. He has no interest in school. He keeps to home. He can bide there and be perfectly happy. He was a scrap seemed like forever. Now he is gone all spindly.

I envy him, I said. He can have a normal childhood. He'll not have the War hangin' over him ... will not have to be a kid one day and a grownup the very next.

How old are you? she said.

Twenty.

I turned 22 last August, she said. I do not feel young any longer.

Me neither, I said.

Long about this time a year, I said, when work is slow, I go rambling. I want my own land. I have not found the property suits me yet, least one I can afford ...

I went some wide of the truth there. I visit friends in the winter, boys from the seminary mostly, but in the Tallahassee area. I am not usually gone from home long. I like to sleep in my own bed. I have a pillow that I favor. I wish I had brought it along.

She accepted what I said—did not take it as some lame excuse for my being in these parts, which is what it amounted to. It was not something I thought on beforehand, nor even as I spoke. It just came out, did not ask permission. She did not seem to think twice on it.

My father was a sutler during the War, I went on. He had a wagon, good mules. He had two set a mules. When he came home he traded off. He followed the troops up in Georgia. He sold tinware, canteens, camp kettles and such. Stationary. Anything from flannels to sweets. He did not hold to peddling gimcracks or trifles. He gave the boys what they needed—bust head whiskey, cheroots.

What you grinnin' at so? she said.

It was one a Pa's jokes. He was not really allowed to sell whiskey. He would get his permit revoked if he had.

A lazy humor took her countenance.

Your daddy was a card, she said. She had a quick little side smile when something amused her.

You got him pegged. The old man was corny, I said. He was known for it.

... Sugar, I continued. Chaw. Notions—needle and thread, buttons. Candles. You name it. There were a couple times when he came home, he brought word a them that did not make it. Boys we knew. I think he put me in school hoping the War would end afore I got to it. We were exempt at the seminary, except for emergencies. His plan almost worked.

I had to tell her a little about the seminary, the cadets, and the fight at Natural Bridge. Then I spoke on about Pa.

He fought against the Seminoles in '57, south a here even, down in the Big Cypress. He signed on with John Bull Parkhill, him and 65 others. Said you could go but a week in the swamp 'fore you got worn out and sick. Hard to find tolerable ground to sleep on he said. Parkhill was killed down there. After Pa came home, he did not want much to do with guns. He saw things that did not set right with him. What they were he kept to himself. He always carried a double barrel in his wagon, not sure he ever loaded it. But he believed in the Cause.

He did not come back when the War ended, I said. I went lookin' for him in Georgia. Macon was the last place we had a letter from. I tracked down his wagon finally in La Grange, near the Alabama border, but the family that had it, bought it from a man across the line. Pa's mules were not with it, but the wagon was his. He had branded it here and there. By then it was not more'n a relic.

Them that owned it were decent folks. They had four little kids, far apart as steps on a ladder. He paid for the wagon, had the bill o' sale. There were not one thing crooked to them.

Then come a big snow storm in LaGrange. That was

new to me. They had me stay with them till it let off.

It was the first time I ever left Florida, an' so far the last. When the snow quit, I felt a need to get on home. Whatever happened to Pa, I reckoned it nothin' good. He made money at what he was doin'. I guess some son of a bitch else figured that out.

She got up and walked inside, came back with Neil Clary's image on a tintype. Neil looked young and hale.

A piece of once was, she said. He was cow huntin' then. When he came around after a drive, we spent time together. I do not know, she said, when he comes home, if I'll recognize him anymore. He'll be a man now.

Neil was clean shaven in the picture, and he was grinning.

I never seen anyone smile at the camera before, I said.

He's a joker, she said. He could not help himself.

You think he'll come back then? I said. It is been some bit a time passed.

I believe we all get one gift. Mine is patience. I say it with more experience than I care to think on.

The missin' him will not go away. It is there, she said. Sometimes it settles, and I can bear with it well enough. Other times it's just a kick in the head.

She stared at the picture.

He had to borrow the suit coat from his brother, Sheldon.

His family's still around? I said.

Only Sheldon. Neil is the youngest of them. Sheldon a year older. He stays out at their farm in Terra Ceia, north of here a little. Their father died ... from lockjaw. The mother went to live with a daughter in Texas. Older brothers and sisters grew up and moved on. I never met them. They were gone time I got here.

Sheldon was hurt up north. I do not recall now exactly where. Virginia? I think it was there. And not in battle, some camp accident. His right leg is crippled. It looks like a bow.

He resembles Neil some in his features and is nothing like him in nature, not now. I bethought him a very decent fella once. But he is bitter. His life ... he is just waiting it out. He is no longer taking part.

I visited once, she said. That was real close to unpleasant. I felt ill-at-ease. He can work himself into a proper fret over nothing at all. He has little good to say, or aught else for that matter. I believe the real problem is, he is there alone, and he does not like himself.

That is gone work at you, I said.

Yes, she said, but ... you cut your cloth. He deserves a right telling off I think. But it needs to come from his betters, not me. I shan't be his scold.

Three big yellow and black butterfly got to weaving around us.

They are called swallowtails, she said. I always wondered how that name came about.

We watched them until they went on.

How did you get down here from home?

I took the train to Cedar Keys, I said. On one of the islands, they call it Sennie Oatie, there's a wild little town, a couple hundred folks. They all sawyers. Logging cedar. I happened to pull in there on payday. The place was hoppin'. I got into it, kicked up the devil a bit. That was good times.

I went to Tampa from there on a river steamer. We were not meant to stop long, but the boat needed work. Tampa is a hard lookin' town.

I like those little steamers, she said. They are quiet. The sternwheelers now, you can hear them thrashing along a mile off.

I went on about Tampa: Three churches and five saloons, far as I explored. All built slipshod. A good many soldiers stationed there. Bluecoats do not set right with me still ... but ... nothin' to do about it. An' they paid me no mind, so ... Oysters and turtle to eat, was all there seemed to be on the bill o' fare. Some mighty fine oysters tho' I have to say. There are gaming tables in the bars—faro, keno, chuck-a-luck. Private rooms for poker. None a that interested me, but they were busy. An' they got a tin pan alley. The music ... it were not much to speak of. But that they had it surprised me. That town was a curiosity.

We were delayed two days an' nights there, then came on down to Manatee village. I took lodging at the Gates' Hotel. I laid up there half the week. Was not much to do, an' that is what I needed. I jes' felt played out from travelin'. I caught a ride with a fisherman o'er to this side finally an' boarded at the Lamb place—that old cabin close on the river bank, squared off logs, sets under six big oaks?

The Lambs not been here long, I said. The Mrs. is expectin'. Mr. Lamb wants to plat the town and call it Palmetto. He stayed busy ... lookin' to buy land mostly. He is interested in live oak timber. They from Mississippi. Came here flush, seems like.

With a sack of gold and another of silver, she said, from what I was told.

I had liked sleeping there I was thinking. Clean and comfortable. A good trundle bed.

I met Lamb, she said. He came by. He was looking for Lee. Kind of dour. Or pensive, maybe. I'll be kind and call him pensive, tho' ... that is going some. Last I heard, I told him, Lee was out to Red Level on business. He wanted no truck with me and Sug. I go now or lose the tide, he said. It was more like he was thinking aloud than talking to us. Then he turned around and walked off. No How d'do when he came, no goodbye, wish-you-well when he left.

He does not say much, not to me surely, I said. I could hardly pry a word loose. He has a son named Dool. He is eight or nine I'd guess. He's a talker. He has five little sisters. I think he liked havin' a feller around to jaw with.

That cabin originally belonged to Madam Joe, she said.

Her last name is Atzeroth, came here from Germany early on. She had lodging and a little store there. Our orange trees come from her. The oranges are Bittersweets. They make really good juice. She got the original seeds from down in Havana. The man who planted our grove lasted five years. He lived in your hut, never got to building a house proper, tho' he cut timber for it ... what turned out to be a big help to Lee. Then he ran out of health and money at the same time.

She had another tintype, of herself, a younger version from New Orleans days. She wore a nice looking day dress with a lace collar, hair in ringlets streaming down over her shoulders.
You look ... right smart, I said. Very becoming.
Thank you, Virgil. As you can see, it was taken before fashion went well-nigh forgotten. My hair was to my ankles then. I was not so sunburnt and freckled.

There was a good-sized stone crock in the shade next to the house. I had seen Sugarbee fooling with it. I asked about it.
What she keep in that? I said.
It's her brine crock. Possum. Squirrel. Coon. Whatever wild thing she catches, we do not have it right away, it stores there. That is some salty dog now. Eat some of that, you have cotton mouth for a good while. But she likes anything reminds her of souse. She eats possum in the winter. She will not in summer. I'll not eat it, period. She has funny tastes. Okra soup ...
I have used okra juice many a time to clean the metal on my guns. I am not so crazy about it as an edible. I did not say this, I thought it.
... goober peas. You got to watch out or she'll make you some periwinkle stew. Those little clams? Hard to get the sand out. That is another dish of hers I am not partial to. Otherwise, she sets a fine table, tho' it is all wild fare.

Tonight we are having squirrel perloo. She snared two of the critters this morning. She uses swamp cabbage in the dish rather than rice, and I prefer it.

Lee bought her a Dutch oven. An' she has that iron grill for to barbecue meat and fish. Oysters. She does up pumpkin on it, too, and sweet corn.

The Dutch oven, I said. That long-legged kettle?

Yes.

It was a deep, round pot, with three legs, longer than most. You could bank a good amount of coals underneath it. The lid was flat, put hot embers on it. Seemed like you could cook most anything in that.

Lee got it from a drummer, came in on one of the big sternwheelers from up north. It looks ancient to me, but he paid a pretty penny. Sug is got a long-legged frying pan too, one of them iron spiders, she makes cornbread in.

She likes to cook, and she is good at it, Miss Mayfield said. She does not think much of my efforts, and mostly will not even let me help.

I was curious about what Sugarbee smoked in her pipe. She had a corn cob pipe with a switch cane stem, had it in her mouth most of the time whether lit or not.

She calls it dimba, Miss Mayfield said. You look at the plant, it's some kind of hemp. She has a big patch of it. The one has that stick fence around it? She got seeds from a boyfriend she had for a time. He was Cuban. She smokes enough, it makes her happy. Anything causes that, I encourage. She grows some tobacco too ... does not need money for that anymore, which is helpful. We go light on boughten things. You have a paper of snuff tho', she'll not turn down a pinch.

Sug is an odd stick, she added. She will let her mind be heard. She'll not bridle her tongue. And there is a fiery side to her—

She keeps that side toward me, I said.

She owns a fair amount of country caution. Takes her

awhile to get used to folks. I mammy-ied up to her after my mother passed.

We took a walk along the river, which curled along its edge and washed the shoreline. Sea grape leaves turning colors, red and yellow. The river looks a mile wide here. Directly across is Shaw's Point and another midden, maybe 150 yards long, more compact and not nearly as big as the one on this side. She told me it is where the Spanish first landed in these parts.
On the way back, we stopped and looked over Sugarbee's kitchen garden. She pointed out cow peas and collards and corn.
The pumpkins and sweet potatoes, she said, need no tending. They are on their own and do well at it.
A sternwheeler passed. We listened to the clacking of the paddles and its rhythmic wheezing—choosh, choosh … Its whistle sounded in a rush of steam, then echoed off the water.

If you feel like staying on a while, there is plenty of work, she said. That pile of sand and oyster shell behind the house, I need a rainwater cistern built. I could use a hand with that. We have that little cistern on the back corner of the house. It is not enough. We get dry spells. We need water, especially in the spring, or the garden gets parched when the plants are but little. We have to fetch it from the pond down there a ways—she motioned toward the west. It is fresh water but not the best. And the pond has a fair share of moccasins.
We take buckets in the boat. It is way too hard. Sug is strong. She can carry a bucket by one hand and a piggin full of water balanced on her head. I have a time with half a bucket.
Do not get the job done now, when the rains come the sand will wash away. And it was too hard gettin' up. Lee built that little kiln for firing bricks when he made the

fireplace. It is primitive but works fine. It could be useful. There are planks around for forms. He left some tools—pickaxe and spade. A hand-barrow. Truly, she said, there is so much to be done just now, I have a sense of bewilderment at times. It seems impossible to work enough hours in a day.

I would like that, I said.

She took a deep breath, and let it out, smiled.

If you stay till full moon in May, it would be of great help to me.

What wages are we talkin'?

Nothing much far as coin, she said. It is scarce and prices high. We hard up and low down on the pole around here. And not just us. About everyone. We do on as little as we can. I dream of the day I can put money by. When the oranges start producing good, we can get two dollars a hundred. The buyer comes and picks for you. She thought a moment. How about room and board? she said. And sterling companionship.

I looked off. I was thinking if I would be needed at home anytime soon. I reckoned not.

We'll make your roof sound ... and repair the mosquito bar. Should change the ticking in your bed, too ... it smells musty.

I was still thinking.

I'll get Sug to be agreeable, she added. Tho', she often does not heed a thing I say. So ... no promises, mind. But I'll try.

Well, that settles it. A bargain then.

We shook hands on it.

When do you suppose, I said, her loving kindness will go into effect?

That afternoon we had silver trout for dinner. When we were done, I threw my scraps to one of Sugarbee's guinea hens that was nearby with her gray-speckled biddies.

Doan, she said.

What?

What chu done. Dey eggs start tastin' fishy.

I looked at Miss Mayfield.

I am working on the bein' nice part, she said.

Hard work followed. I spent the entire first week grubbing out roots in the cistern spot. The midden was made up of conch, oyster, clam and scallop shell, limestone rock, sand, and untold centuries of rotted wood and leaves falling on it. I needed several men and a boy for help. All I had was my two hands. Thankfully you did not have to be skilled labor to do tabby work. Lee had left a square, level, plumb bob, and Miss Mayfield made a drawing of what she had in mind.

To make the concrete was simple enough: equal parts lime, sand, shell, water. I had to chop oak for the kiln. And I soon took to cutting all the wood that Sugarbee needed for cooking.

I had to burn shell to extract lime from shells and green oak ashes. Stoking the fire was pleasant early mornings when I first started, when mornings were still cool. As time went on and the weather warmed, it turned into hot work.

You need to mix the wet tabby concrete good, make a slurry of it and shovel it into the form. Add shell. Ram it all into the form. The forms were two parallel planks extending the full length of the wall, shorter boards on the ends. Let it dry a couple, three days, depending on the weather. Remove the form, the boards moved up as each layer of tabby dried. Then start over. Your hands get cut and roughed up and poisoned.

I made the walls 20 inches wide. Two-thirds of the cistern was below ground. My first batch made all of about a square foot of concrete. Sugarbee came by, stared at it, looked at me and walked away. The fice came by and looked at it, raised a leg. Some guinea hens blinked at it a moment or two, then started potracking. But I got better at the job. I worked out a routine. I kept at it.

The cistern connected to the house held a thousand gallons, made of cypress staves held together by iron hoops. What I had going would be at least three times as big, maybe more. The roof of the house was good red cedar shake. I needed some kind of eave trough to route the water off the roof and into the cistern. You could make gutters out of cypress. They will last. But I would need to get the cypress cut. I needed plaster. I needed some kind of lid for the cistern, probably just make one of wood. I would figure all that out later. Now was time for back breaking labor and little else. Pa had an old-fashioned word for this kind of work: moil. Work that is no fun, that you just slog through best you can.

Was not many days into this I noticed a welt on top of my left wrist, which soon developed into a marble-sized lump. It did not hurt particularly, but it was annoying and certainly ugly. I showed it to Miss Mayfield.

A Bible bump, she said. Get Sug to look at it. She takes care of such. I'm going down shortly. I'll tell her.

She smiled for some reason. I detected a bit of mischief in that smile but did not think too much on it at the time.

I got busy at something or other but a bit later came across Sugarbee at the table with two conch. She had already taken the meat out of the shell.

How you clean it? I said.

Cut away ev'ryting ain't white, she said. She finished up quickly with that, beat them with a wooden mallet a bit, and threw them into a bucket of water.

Let me see what wrong wit you, she said.

I showed her my wrist.

Fetch yer Bible, she said.

I went and got the Bible out of my tote. I removed Neil's ring and set it aside.

Sit down. Hand on de table flat, Sugarbee said.

I did so.

She laid the Book on my wrist.

Be a li'l demon inside. Bible chase hit away. Close yer eyes, she said.

I felt her raise the Bible off my wrist. Then she slammed it down what seemed like hard as she could.

Damn it! I said. That smarts!

She smiled. I guess it was the first time I saw her do that, a quick disarming smile. Some mischief there, too.

Gone feel better when de hurt stop, she said.

I favored that hand for some days when I worked and before long forgot to. The bump kept getting smaller. In two weeks it had disappeared.

There was a lean-to shed attached to the back of the house where they kept provisions, Sugarbee's cooking utensils, food safe, wash tubs, tools, odds and ends. In it I found Lee's foot adz and draw knife that he used to square the logs to the house, a mallet and chisels to cut out mortise pockets. A shake ax. That had all been a hard bit of work. He left the tools sharp, but he left them behind, I got to thinking, because he did not ever want to see them again.

We got up at sunrise, bed at twilight, sometimes later—10, 12 hour days of work in between. First thing in the morning I built up the kitchen fires, washed my face. Once a week I shaved. Sugarbee did the washing on Mondays, took clothes and washboard to the riverside. On Mondays also she cooked red bean soup and made ash cakes. Since I knew a week had passed by these things, I shaved then.

We would have a big breakfast—guinea eggs, cornbread, sweet potato, coffee. And not much until dinner in early afternoon. We ate then whatever Sugarbee had been stewing all day. Or catch some fish and do them up. Pick oysters from one of the many bars. Our evening meal was light and mainly what was left-over from dinner. You were all but too tired to eat by then. Times in between meals I would come by and see what was in the food safe, usually sweet potato and cornbread, take a bite or two, have cold coffee or honey water. After supper we sat around the plank table and drank coffee and one by one went off to bed.

Alone at the table, twilight, the shadows gone mosaic, I watched the river turning dark.

Sometimes, before I go to sleep, I'll see the light of Miss Mayfield's candle-lantern and wonder about her. She has been kind to me in many ways. She is keen-witted. Even-tempered. I have not once seen her fly off the handle. She displayed plain common sense, and toward both Sugarbee and myself, a great deal of forbearance. She was all in all perfectly normal but for the fact she thought Neil Clary would someday return to her. It seemed a kind of specific madness. I found it unsettling, not least of all for the secret I kept. She must know, deep down, I thought, that he is residing in eternity now. Still, you would notice her eyes on the river. See a boat. *Who is it?*

She was not the only woman that waited, I knew, just one of the last.

One day, Easter Sunday was mentioned. When it came, the women put on black calico dresses. Sugarbee wore an elaborate indigo head rag. She called it a *tignon*. Miss Mayfield a straw bonnet. I have not said much about what Ella Mayfield looked like, but seeing her that morning dressed up and her hair braided, bone hairpins, I thought her fine as crème gravy. Just right down pretty.

They waited for the incoming tide and left in the row boat headed for Manatee village and a church meeting. They took a bucket of food. I had written a letter to my family telling them about my trip and where I was at present, and sent it along with them to post. I stayed and rested. Every muscle in my body ached.

I was sitting at the table looking out to the river that

forenoon. I had a plate with some sweet potato left on it, when a blue jay landed on my shoulder. It startled me a bit, I braced up some, but did not brush him off or do anything quick. I stayed quiet enough, as he seemed to know what he was up to. I turned my head a little to view him. He spoke a couple things in my ear before he hopped down and started eating potato scraps from the plate. I would rate him a fairly messy eater. No table manners whatsoever. When he was full, he looked at me sort of intently, maybe trying to place me, lolled his head side to side a couple times, and flew off.

The women returned that evening. I asked what the preacher had to say.

Chaff, Miss Mayfield said. Did not amount to a hoot. I found no balm in it. A bunch of humbug. Hectorin'. Maledictions. *The days of wrath are nigh!* Some folks like that sort of thing. I do not. And I kept thinking, The wrath has been here and gone, fool, did you not notice?

Sugarbee was sitting there. A might loud, she said. An' comes along like hit all fell out his haid.

I go for some society, Miss Mayfield said. You talk to the preacher one on one now, he will parse every word you say. He was very interested in who you are exactly.

How'd he know about me?

The grapevine, she said. The river talks. And it is long-winded.

What you tell him?

I changed the subject, she said. I am not into chatting with him in the first place. He does not improve on closer acquaintance. Besides, the man is a Yankee lover. It is none of his damn concern who you are.

My eyes cut toward her on that. She had some expressions she used: tarnation, dickens and such-like. But this was first time I heard her cuss. Truth be told, it was the first I heard a woman cuss since the last time I was in a brothel.

The service was held in a pretty place, Miss Mayfield said, down by the mineral spring.

What sort a preacher is he?

Methodist, she said. A journeyman. He'll be in Sarasota next Sunday or out to Red Level.

Sugarbee said, We cat lick anyways.

I squinted at her. I looked at Miss Mayfield

Catholics, she said.

I told Miss Mayfield later: A jaybird landed on my shoulder this afternoon. He seemed awfully friendly.

He is one of Sug's pets, she said. A crow stole him from his nest and dropped him at Sug's feet. For some reason it did not kill him, just knocked him for a loop. She raised him. He is gone wild, but stops by for a handout now and then. That was a surprise I would think.

It was, I said.

Toward the end of April, a good rain lasted most of the day. When it let up, I got a hand line rigged out and went fishing. I was soon into a school of reds that seemed half the river wide. I caught reds till my forearms were want to give out. They were all around 15 pounds. I kept the last two. I cleaned them and gave them to Sugarbee to cook. She added cornbread and pokeberry greens, and we had a feast at sunset, the light gone low and moody, great flocks of birds following the river back to their roosts.

We sat at the table by the kitchen fire most evenings after supper, the weather still pleasant, cool breeze off the river, a pine torch burning. Miss Mayfield would sew or read, Sugarbee readying food for in the morning. Or she fooled with her seeds or plaited palmetto hats. She whittled clothespins, skewers from cedar she used for grilling, sharpened palings for her garden fence. She was never in a hurry but kept always busy. Someone had given her a laurel root. From time to time she carved at it, trying to make a fancy pipe. She seemed often in a wayward mood, something not accounted for. You sort of got used to it.

We had cornbread with nearly all our meals. Miss Mayfield said they still had to buy cornmeal, could not grow enough. The corn they planted was for roasting ears, which we had begun partaking of. If there was cornbread left over from supper, we might put honey on it and have that with a bowl of coffee. Or sometimes Sugarbee popped corn. We talked, mostly recounting the small events of the work day. If no one said much, that also was cordial and good as the talking. When Sugarbee got in a good mood from smoking dimba, she would spin yarns. These resembled tall tales or fables. A good many of them were simply impenetrable, and I at times found it hard to keep a straight face. She might start off like so: I ain't know how dis story acquired hits origination, but …

This night Sugarbee went to bed early. Since she was gone, we talked about her.

She had skinned a raccoon earlier and left it hanging. Anything that got near her garden was liable to end up on our table.

How will she cook it? I said.

She'll put some sweet potatoes around him and parboil him and then bake the lot. It tastes like dark meat chicken, only greasier and more tender.

She locks up tight at night, I said.

She does. Keeps the ghosts away. She has some strange notions on all that.

How so?

Well, for instance … it is her belief that when the body dies, the soul goes on dreamin'.

She went on: She talks of voodoun occasionally, whatever that is exactly. Some New Orleans malarkey. I do not ask, nor want to know. She believes in Jesus and Mother Mary, too. Wants to get it all covered I guess. Believes there is a good God, the bon Dieu, and a bad, but the bad is not the devil, that is something else. Far as I can tell, the bad one is of no great import, seems to be in charge of tomfoolery and the like. She is dead-level sure her bon

Dieu smokes a pipe. I do not know how she arrives at these things. Believes if a hant is inclined to mischief and gives you too much trouble ... and say you know who the hant belongs to ... you need to dig up the grave and kill 'im again. I think the spectral world is just as real to her as this one.

I saw her out in the dimba garden one night, she said, 't was a full moon. I walked down to make sure it was her and not a hant. I have never seen one of them. But, no ... there was Sug, her face covered in ash. She looked right through me. Then ran off into the woods. I never asked her about it, and she never said. And I just have no idea what that was all about.

Believes in the rougouroo, she added.

The what?

Well, she explained that a rougouroo is a gator-man. Or a gator that turned into a man and could turn back again. There were aspects of the creature that remained murky. It was Louisiana swamp lore and nonsense to me.

So one evening as the three of us sat around the table, I said to Sugarbee, I heard a gator croakin' down by the pond.

She turned her head quick.

It were either gator or a rougouroo, not certain which.

Doan speak dat name aloud, she said. Hit gone bring 'im on.

Can you kill one a them? I said.

Not but wit silver, she said. Doan let 'im see what chu up to neither, be quick ... or he put a coyse on you. Rob yer strength. Make you dry up like a ol' dead a' range.

Silver? I said.

Yeh. An best you git 'im at a crossroads. Dey weak at a crossroad somehow.

I wonder why that is?

Doan know. Now afore you go lookin' for hit, 't is best to cut a johnny conqueroo in half.

A johnny conqueroo?

Hit a yam … someting like … only wit powers.

Good to get all that cleared up, I said.

Most folks think the Yella Jack comes by boat or train, Miss Mayfield said, or in the mail. Sug thinks the rougouroo to blame. She sceered of it.

Live an' larn, Sugarbee said. She lit her pipe, shook her head up and down a bit. I's not sayin' owt else on dat.

Miss Mayfield invited me into her house one evening. I had been inside during the day, not at night. This was to be one of the last cool evenings before summer got into swing.

The inside is composed of a single large room. There was a snug fire going in the tabby fireplace. Candles lit. Work clothes hung on pegs along one wall. A little foot tub. A four-poster bed with a mosquito bar. The four-poster was not of the fancy variety. There was nothing fancy here. A white pitcher and wash basin on a little sideboard and a bowl full of speckled guinea eggs on a shelf above. A small looking-glass hanging. Books on the fireplace mantel. An inkwell, quill and sander there as well. A little coffee mill to grind beans. A clock that was broken. It was the only timepiece on the property.

There was a rocker and a straight back chair, the same rocker that usually sat on the porch. Wide pine plank flooring. The walls whitewashed. A stair ladder set off to one side against a wall that led to the attic, unfinished still, bare rafters and but a small loft for storage. She meant at some point to make it into a sleeping loft that would cover half the room. There was a small glass window on each side of the front door, the panes thick and full of air bubbles, maybe a foot high and two long, and on the west wall where the wind blew strongest against, two shutter windows. It was a simple house and comfortable to be in.

I picked up one of her books, a collection of poetry, and

glanced through it—saw the names Henry Timrod, Sidney Lanier, Edgar Allen Poe. I knew of Poe's reputation more than his work. The other two I had not heard of. We studied military tactics at the seminary. History, topography, the physical sciences. We had composition courses. And those of another sort, such as surveying, which I liked quite a lot, as I did the practical everyday part of our studies, drill and marksmanship.

They taught us grammar and penmanship. Our instructor was good at punctuation and grammar and taught me well enough. There is a sense of ordering to it that I liked. He was good with penmanship also, but I did not get on to that and scrawl to this day. Far as literature, we studied the classics and most all had warfare in them. Homer's *Iliad* was a favorite. Other than the *Iliad*, they were not much into poems. What little we read I would have to label inspirational and not of enough interest to me that I could recall the names of who wrote them.

At home we have few books—the Bible, McGuffey readers, an old *Webster's Unabridged Dictionary*. Words interest me. They have a specific meaning, more or less. The Bible I find a trial for the most part. I have my God. I pray, as He is worthy of talking to. And might be it is a mistaken notion on my part, but I believe at least now and again that He is listening. These facts do not help me with the Bible any or really have much to do with it. I prefer reading Webster, tho' I failed to mention this to Miss Mayfield. I have said it aloud a couple times in the past and got curious looks in return.

After a while she brought forth a letter from Neil Clary. She adjusted her pince-nez. They were nickel-rimmed.

Cheaters, she said of them.

It is the last letter I got from him. I hardly got so many to begin with. Neil can not read or write. This one was written for him by a army preacher, Chaplain McNeilly. The letter came from near a place called Ezra Church, she said, dated July 28th, 1864.

When she said Ezra Church, I recalled that Neil had spoken of it. The church is located some three miles west out Lickskillet Road from Atlanta. What he said was, during that fight it came clear to him that General Hood intended on getting him killed. Hood was reckless with his troops, he was headlong. Neil had started taking it personal. They fought three times in the 10 days since Hood had taken over for General Joe Johnston, many good men lost in each battle. I knew now that there were near 3,000 Southern casualties at Ezra Church alone. And after Ezra Church, he understood how things would end for him if he stayed on. So he lit out.

He started walking home, headed southwest, followed the railroad tracks into Alabama. He stayed the month of October at an abandoned farm, everything in place except the folks that owned it and their stock. He found side meat in a store house, a cask of molasses half full. It is what he ate that month, pork fat and blackstrap. He remembered it fondly. That month was the best he had of it on his journey.

He walked on, eventually all the way down to the coast before he cut east to Florida. Walked a fair piece, he said. He stayed away from towns, from people for the most part, stuck to the by-roads and pathless woods. Over time tho' he came across men doing the same as he was.

I picked up on what Miss Mayfield was saying at the end of the letter:

… Nearly dark. We are bivouacked beside a cemetery. It is fitten. This day we charged six times into a strong Yankee line. They were on a ridge fortified with rails and logs, and pews taken from the Ezra Church meeting house. They murdered us. The boys refused to charge a seventh time. I do not know how much grit I have left for this. I hope we meet up again ere long. My love, as always.

Without your man, you pine, she said. It cuts at you.
I refuse to think of him in some far away cemetery in

a lonely grave marked *Rebel Unknown*. I want him to live out his days, even if not with me. I want him to have a good life and a good death.

The full moon of May came and went, and I was not nearly done with the cistern. I agreed to stay on until the job was finished.
When Sugarbee learned of this, she stopped me.
Too much hem-hawin' now, she said. Do you know what chu doin'?
You are too pert spoken, I said.
Well? she said.
No, I said. I know not.

The next morning as Sugarbee was preparing breakfast she said, Dere a painter come by las' night.
A panther? I said.
Yeh.
You saw it?
No. I's inside.
You heard it?
No. He marked.
On your place?
Not on't. Nigh about. My spells shied 'im away.
I did not hear the fice bark.
Feist wit Miss Ella. He good at snakes an' rats. Not no painter, no ... he want to sleep tru dat.

I tracked the cat for a while where he walked the shoreline. Found scat. Looked a young one by the prints. He found the compost piles, played there some. Then he headed toward the cut. They've been near hunted out around home, but when I was a child I many a time heard their yowl in the night. It has a human quality and is fairly unsettling. This one had been quiet, not sure of the territory maybe and feeling his way.

One late afternoon a small sailboat pulled up to shore. Gulls followed the boat in, just a-screaming. A man carried a basket up to the house. He was big, dark red/brown from sun, a week's worth of frosted stubble on his face. He looked to be from a rough neck of the woods. Turned out he was a friend to Sugarbee, a fisherman called Chago. She surprised me by speaking a little Spanish with him.

She had that Cuban boyfriend, Miss Mayfield said. She picked up their lingo some. Tho' I am thinking she is no great shakes at it. Her version may be peculiar as her English. Chago's his replacement I guess. He is workin' it, part time at least. He has means. A nice boat anyway. She looked at Sugarbee. Why anyone would want that cranky ole thing, she said, is beyond me.

The fisherman brought Loggerhead eggs he'd gathered over at Anna Maria, a long island close by to the west. Sugarbee put a pot of water to boiling, added a hefty portion of salt, and after a while we sat around and ate turtle eggs. The whites of the eggs never solidified. The yolk did. We knocked off the tops and ate them from the shell. They are small. I had a dozen myself.

At some point, the fisherman said something to Sugarbee and gestured toward me.

You remind 'im o' someone, she said.

Who?

He disremembers.

She thought on it a moment or two.

Someone he ain't like too much …

She found that pretty funny. Got a kick out of it.

When the sun went low, Chago made to leave. We all walked down to his boat.

What you call that? I said to Miss Mayfield.

A Melonseed skiff, she said.

The boat was a two-seater, the sail wrapped around the mast. Chago freed it and was ready to go. He rowed out into the wind, then took off fast to the west.

Those Melonseed, Miss Mayfield said, they are well-behaved in the wind. If the wind is not up, they row nice. 'T would not surprise me if I had my own someday.

You a dreamer, cher, Sugarbee said.

I woke the next morning long before dawn, a mockingbird just singing away. I decided to take the day off, the first one since I got here. I announced my intentions at breakfast.

I want to explore the island, I said. I'll be gone a spell.

There were only two other inhabitants lived on the island then, a negro couple.

Sugarbee said something about their dogs. Something neutral, like, Dey have dawgs.

I'd heard them baying at times. She did not mention, however, as she might have, how big-headed and nasty they were.

Where they live?

Yon, she said and flicked her hand backwards. Take de shotgun, she said. You see anyting be good eatin' … I's tired a fish. Tired a conks, too. She handed me the powder flask and shot pouch.

I had started going barefoot by this time. I walked the shoreline out to the point where the river meets the Gulf, the water blue and turquoise, sea grass like green ribbons on the bottom. At low tide, fiddler crabs gathered in the flats by the thousands. There were tarpon rolling out a ways, 100-pound silver minnows. The water in close was alive with redfish, trout, mackerel, snook. One snook passed by so large I thought it a shark coming for me.

I waded in, up past my knees. A baby manatee nudged me from behind. Not knowing right off what it was, I nearly walked on the water out of there. He just hung around me for a while. He wanted to play.

I got to thinking about Ella Mayfield. Sometimes as we are talking, she'll go away, her eyes on nothing in this world—then shortly come back like she had been with me all along. I got to thinking about the cavities in my teeth. She told me about a dentist across the river who is stone deaf. If you got to yelling when he worked on you, he could not hear it. I was thinking about that coffee she favored, a brand called Arbuckle. My thoughts were all over the place.

I threw my fishing line. After a while I hooked on to something too big for me to deal with. I fought hard but did not gain on it at all. My hands started getting cut up. Finally, it threw the hook and just as well. It did not get near the surface. I never saw what it was.

I continued wading around the point and past it, then ran into mangroves on my right and deep water to the left. I paddled along with one arm, the other holding the gun and powder high, and turned in at a little cove until I found bottom again, walked out of the water, sat there for a time.

I cut inland. It was rough going through mangroves, but I came to some clear grassy areas, small salt ponds, then more woods, big timber now, old live oaks.

The first dog came across me when I was up a limb on a grandfather oak, just looking around. The oak had to be 200 years old, maybe more. One of the lower branches swayed to about five feet from the ground. I had climbed up. So he did not have to tree me. I was already there. He had a old dried up fish in his mouth. He put it down and howled bloody murder. When the other two dogs came, he picked up the fish again. The shotgun was down below leaned against the trunk.

Who these dogs belong to? I hollered. Hey, whose dogs are these?

An elderly negro man with bad pox marks on his face walked up. He had a musket, antique and rusty, but … still worked good enough I would think.

Dawgs hungry, he said.

It seemed the case. You could count their ribs.

How 'bout gettin' them under control, I said.

He snapped his fingers, and they shut up and started scratching.

Virgil Hill, I said.

Proud to know ye, he said. He talked slowly, laboring the words so, you felt as tho' you were making your way through porridge.

Where'r you come from? he said.

I stay over to the Mayfield place.

My regards to 'em.

I surely will mention that.

Lawd's blessin' on 'em.

I'll tell them that, too.

Doan got any cornbread about ye by chance? he said.

No, I said.

You favor gull eggs? he said.

Gull eggs?

Lee use ter buy gull eggs from me.

I did not bring any money along, I said.

Ye got any chaw?

No, I do not. I'll make sure I bring some next time I come by.

See dat ye do, suh, he said. And he and the dogs moseyed away.

Why you old son of a bitch, I said. I had not spoken very loud. It would not have seemed polite.

I stopped by a little fresh water pond on the way back and killed two curlew. I got both with one shot, as they just sat there trying to figure out what in the world I happened to be. I thought I smelled deer in one area but searched for sign and found none. Then I came across a sow with piglets and shot one of them. I found an old lightning-struck pine and packed some fatwood splinters. Miss Mayfield and Sugarbee were sitting at the table when I came in with my load. I handed over the prizes to Sugarbee.

We heard you shootin', Miss Mayfield said.

Tiens, tiens! Sugarbee said. How 'bout dat!

I believe there is a compliment in there, Miss Mayfield said, if you hunt it down.

You run into dem folks? Sugarbee said.

The man, yeh.

Name be Pernell. He doan tawk right.

He worked for Lee awhile on the house, Miss Mayfield said, riving shingles mostly. Lee paid him in food. He is just full of playful banter, ain't he?

I missed that part, I said.

His wife doan tawk at all. Her a gator neck, Sugarbee said.

She has a goiter, Miss Mayfield said.

I never did spot their house, I said.

Thatch and driftwood, she said, all ramshackled together. Hide doors. And so covered with vines, nigh impossible to see lest you right up on the thing. The Yankees took a long while to find it, but them folks had nothing to steal to begin with.

Do you ever visit? I said.

F'why? Sugarbee said. She seemed taken aback.

We ate about everything there was of the pig except the little hooves and snout and tail. Sugarbee put them in her brine crock. The next morning we cut up pieces of intestine and tied them to string, and the three of us caught a bucketful of blue crabs.

Late May, early June, the weather turned steamy. The sky leaden and growling late in the day. Lightning blinked in the cloud cover. Then rain. Riverboat traffic slowed considerably. So did our work schedule, as around noon the sun sprang into some further ignition.

One evening after rain had cooled things off and a nice wind blew in from the Gulf, we sat at the table after supper. Sugarbee was scouring a pot with wet sand. We had a torch blazing and smudge fires smoking.

What is Tallahassee like? Miss Mayfield said.

A pretty town, I said. Even nicer when I was little. There used to be a waterfall down by the train depot. Twenty, thirty-foot tall ... a pool at the bottom of it. In '57 I think it was, the railroad started laying tracks eastward. They cut across Adams Street, right south of the waterfall, and ended up destroying it.

Why would they do such a thing?

It was in their way, I said.

Good Lord, she said.

A little later, she went on.

I about visited there one time. Leastways I thought on it real serious. This was a year after the War ... maybe less. They had a soldier there I heard about. The story was from an old article in a Tallahassee paper, The Sentinel. All we get here is old news. I heard it secondhand from Mary Gates in the village. She has a little library at the hotel, what reading material her guests leave. One of the guests had the paper just then, and we could not locate her. But Mary said when the Yankees took over they found this fella in a Reb hospital. Nobody at the hospital knew who he was. Nor did he.

I remember that, I said. Some of it. He had not been wounded—

No. Just lost in the mind. It troubled me. I could not imagine to be done that way—to have your mind so mangled entire. He was said to be tall, Mary remembered, 6 foot 2 or so. And I had this wild thought it might be Neil. Did not make sense, first of all, that he would be in Tallahassee. But I could not shake the idea that he was.

Sugarbee stopped cleaning her pot.

A sma' screw loose, what 't was, she said.

Miss Mayfield gave her a wry look.

You not right den, Sugarbee said. You nigh out o' yer head ... be on de outskoyts.

Enough now. Quit saucin'. You about to rile me, Miss Mayfield said.

Uh-oh, Sugarbee said. I's gettin' sceered. I's got the

quavers. She started vibrating wildly.

When you shake your head like that, Miss Mayfield said, I can hear it rattle.

Anyway … long story shortened … I finally got hold of the paper next time we went to the village and read the article. They had this fella at between 35 and 40 years of age. That ruled out Neil. And luckily, I had not gone up there and made a dang fool of myself.

I backfilled around the cistern that morning and found in the dirt a little rust-colored piece of coral with a hole in the center. It appeared worked by human hand, long ago I would think, and looked like a ring. I had cleaned it up earlier. Now I dunked the coral in water to make the colors come alive and showed it to Miss Mayfield.

You can have it, I said.

Thank you, she said. How pretty. This rusty coral has a name. I am not recalling it just now, she said. I want to say … jert? That might be it.

Sugarbee looked at it closely.

Puddin' stone, she said.

Miss Mayfield stared at her.

Why you do like that? she said.

Do what? Sugarbee said.

Make like you know what you talkin' about.

Is it a ring? I said.

Most likely from a necklace, she said, or bracelet.

Sugarbee took the coral from her and examined it, held close to her eye.

Puddin' stone, she reaffirmed.

Gawd, Miss Mayfield said. You are just so chock-full of it …

The bottom part of the cistern was finished. I can not say I'd been exactly giving it hell on this job of late. I stood around looking at the thing some in the mornings, then found better things to do, like hunting or fishing.

But now I had to figure out how to make the lid. I'd do so with wood I reckoned, tho' I did not have any boards except the planks I used to form with, just shot at this point. I had been emptying the cistern, as it started collecting rainwater and wiggle-tails. I tired of that and went to the pond and caught some minnows and put them in it. I was thinking how I might fashion a makeshift lid with palmetto fronds, jimmy-rig it some way or another for the time being, when there was a commotion out front. I had a look.

A big sailboat anchored off shore. Three men in a rowboat were coming toward us, a white man, and two negroes pulling oars. There were three others remained on the sailboat. Miss Mayfield seemed to know who they were, so I went back to the cistern.

A bit later she introduced me to the white man.

Virgil, she said, this is Jonah Coyle.

Virgil Hill, I said and we shook hands, tho' it seemed to pain him some.

He wore a wide-brimmed straw hat, white linen shirt and trousers. He had dressed up for the occasion apparently. He had a fancy walking stick. It seemed an ornament, as he did not limp that I noticed, nor did it ever touch the ground. I took it for a sword-cane finally. How top-notch. He had a black beard, a little gray mixed in. He looked in his 30s, maybe half way through them. He held himself oddly rigid.

Miss Mayfield explained to him that I built the cistern, the problem we were having figuring out a lid and so on. He listened. He had one of his negroes take measurements. His negroes were very black, stout as mules and looked at you straight on.

Good to meet you, he said.

The same, I said, and they all walked away.

Later on Miss Mayfield spoke to me about Jonah Coyle.

He and his family were sugar planters before the War, she said. He has land up river. He is raising cattle now. An' started on an orange grove. Not sure how much he owns of his place and how much the Tallahassee bank share is. I believe he wants to court me, she added.

Did not know how to answer that one, so I kept quiet.

I could have said he looked a haughty son of a bitch, a dandy swell, that he rode a high horse, but did not.

I am not minded to go along with it, she said. It is just him and his negroes, and not so many of them left now. Those boys go with him wherever he goes. Something awkward in that. Mostly, tho' ... the main problem as I see it ... I do not believe he knows how to have any fun.

The cane, I said. Was he in the War?

He was a *druther*, she said.

What's that?

He would druther as not fight, she said. He had a bad limp back then. He hobbled around. After the War, his leg got well mighty easy.

He was shamming? I said.

Believe so, she said. Now he seems spry enough, has a little strut about him, did you notice? Kind of stiff at it, but ...

I had noticed.

The next afternoon, the sailboat returned. Two negroes rowed ashore with seven long, wide boards of heart pine and pitch to seal.

I felt vexed the rest of the day. Sugarbee took note.

A sull's come o'er you, she said. Stop mopin'.

Coyle sent along some manatee meat that Sugarbee grilled for supper. I had not eaten manatee before and was in for a surprise. It tasted much like beef.

Midway through June, maybe 7:00 in the evening, a green color to the air after a short rain. Miss Mayfield says there is another season here before the fall.

They call it High Summer in Louisiana, she said. I call

it jungle season here. The Yella Jack comes then, if it is going to.

I had New Orleans on my mind this morning. It kept popping up for some reason. I ordered some good cloth from there, gray Janes, I was going to make Neil a coat with. It never came. That's what started it, when I thought of that. Then I could not get it to leave me alone.

Can I borrow your Bible for an evening? she said later. There are parts of it I like to read, sort of need to occasionally. Ecclesiastes ... Solomon's Song ...

Sure, I said.

Are you religious, Virgil?

So-so.

I am ... now and then, she said. The War took its toll. I spent a fair amount of faith then for sure. When I was little, tho' ... I'd read the Bible through by my sixth birthday.

Damn! I said. Ah ... shit ...

She smiled at me.

Sorry, I said. I did not mean to sound so—

Common?

Yes.

I've heard worse, she said. Neil swore like a muleteer.

That is a lot to handle for a six-year-old, I said. Not sure how well I could read at that age.

I dreamed of becoming a nun, she said, most Catholic girls do. We went to the Jesuit church on Baronne Street. But there were Angeline nuns in the French Quarter that interested me. They had a school for Creole girls. I liked what they were doing. I would bake cookies and go down there, and talk to them.

About the Bible? I said

Some, yes. But they liked to gossip, too. They could gab. There was only one of them spoke English. She translated for me.

Something tickled her.

I think, probably, when they saw me they thought, Here comes that little girl with the cookies. They were crazy about my cookies.

The women in my family, I said, are devout. Ma and sis and my aunts. 'T will surprise me at times how much so. They can go a little overboard at meetin's. They get into it. Pa only went one time that I recall. He was not so impressed. He spent the sermon rolling his eyes.

I liked the picnics afterwards mostly, I said. But I am not a scoffer. I have my beliefs. They are simple, and there are not so many. No church is needed to hold them.

The reason I have the Book, I said, is I got in trouble once at school and was kicked out for a time. Ma gave me the Book and made me promise to read it. She felt I needed guidance. She wanted me to read it cover to cover. I have not come close to that. I take it with me when I travel, think I'll get to it better then. Does not always work out that way.

I like to read the Psalms, I said. I read Revelation time to time, jes' ... I am not sure why exactly. I can not make head nor tail of it, and that for some reason makes me want to keep delvin' into it.

Catholics call that book The Apocalypse.

It seems a better name, I said. It certainly has not revealed much to me.

What sort of trouble you get into? Did you make bad marks?

I always made good grades. I have no problem with book learnin'. It is easy for me. Workin' things out in the world takes me longer, seems like. No, I said, it was horseplay got me in trouble. Cuttin' up. And I let it go at that.

What happened was I got in a fight with another student, Jesse McKellen, over a girl. She was a planter's daughter. She was pretty, and charming to be with, and spoiled. We both came enamored of her at the same time. We had dress parade at the seminary one Saturday and a frolic afterwards, that she and her older sister attended. Her sister was portly. I was hoping Jesse thought well of portly girls and would let me have this one to myself, but he saw things same as me. We both got lovesick over her. Honestly, I felt like I had a fever when I was near her. And in short order, about three weeks, me and Jesse thought each other a hindrance.

We started railing at each other over a game of muggins one day, got hot-headed and had at it. It was a hard-fought tussle, busted lips and black eyes and bloody noses endured, and we had both been sent home a fortnight, really just long enough for to mend and get back to looking normal again. Jesse had gotten in the best punch of the bout, the last one, a roundhouse left hook wherein he broke his hand on my forehead. It felt like he hit me with a hammer. It did not knock me down, but did impart a bit of wisdom, and I said, Jess, what are we doin'? Somethin' hurtful, he replied. He was shaking his hand. You have a hard head, Virgil. And that was the end of it.

Captain Johnson asked, You did such damage to each other over a game of dominoes? He was skeptical, and rightly. He looked us over and commented, I see nary a winner in this sorry business. And, like I said, sent us home. Afterwards we found out this girl did not give a damn about either one of us. I had been friends with Jesse before the fight and friends again after. The fight quelled the madness. Before it, I wanted him gone to hell on the next thing smoking. It had all been so mean I did not feel like providing details to Miss Mayfield, and so did not.

I finished the lid to the cistern. It came out nice. Black-headed green parakeets on Sugarbee's sunflowers at mid-morning. The wind had been coming out of the west the past three days, storms along the Gulf early on. It was a difficult time. I needed to leave, I did not want to. I started cutting firewood to sell to the steamboats, see if we could make enough money to buy piping to run rain from the roof to the cistern. It was my excuse for the time being.

I was washing myself off in the river that afternoon and

watched a sailboat go past toward the village. A 30-footer, two big sails. A stout man in the stern holding the tiller, a small sail there behind him. A bunch of young kids sat with their legs hanging off the side, the oldest maybe seven or eight. They all looked sunburnt. They waved, and I waved back. A good boat, I commented to myself, solidly built. You could go places in that.

Two of Jonah Coyle's negroes came by at noontime several days later with a written invitation to visit his plantation on the 4th of July, that Saturday. A boat would be sent for Miss Mayfield early in the morning. Sugarbee would go, it was understood. I was not mentioned in the invitation. And I had no desire for it, invited or not. The only way I could suffer through such an event would be to get barking-mad drunk, and I knew that would not end well.

The women heated a flat iron on the stones of a fire circle and ironed their Sunday best.

We did not even consider the 4th during the War, Miss Mayfield said when they had finished. I still do not think well of the flag … but it is a time-honored day … and a celebration of other rebels from long ago.

It's not the day of Jubilee it was when I was little, I said.

No, she said. That it's not. Hard to say when we'll be back. A couple days most likely.

Coyle's men brought along peanut butter pie as a gift, which we had that evening after supper. We all had a slice. Too sweet, too much sugar. I took a small bite and, when I thought nobody was looking, gave the rest to the dog. He made short work of it.

After a time, Miss Mayfield caught my eye.

I saw that, she said.

She touched my hair. It was stiff with salt. I had bathed in the river after work, as I did every day. She took a bucket to the house cistern and came back with it half full. She brought soap.

Here, she said, let me wash your hair. It is turning white.

And she did so. I was hoping for her to do it right down tenderly, but she scrubbed my head like Ma used to when I was a kid.

On the 4th, pink curlews standing in their reflection in still water near dusk. Scattered gunfire up and down the river in celebration. It continued off and on for hours. Terrible tree frog racket. They were trying to coax the rain, but it would not come. I had plenty of time alone to think. The midden is a different place at night, star bright, haunted.

I mulled. I ruminated. Things tugged at me—some I am well aware of, others I can not say or know, could only guess at if I wanted to. I was out of fix truly, as I do not fare well left to my own reflection. I find it difficult to harness the wayward parts. I turn it all over in my mind, and things get to tying in a knot. It seems impossible to go back or onward. I am stuck in thought. I dwell there in an addled way, having an argument with myself, and can not for the life of me fathom which side I am on.

The moon rose. I built up the fire and popped corn. Our pecans get big from late June on into July. I might well be needed to go watch that happen. You do not have to think at home, and that was bully. At another moment I said to myself, I would as lief stay here as not. I'd grown fond of this place. Whatever you believe in, you get close to it here. But I had stayed beyond proper bounds, it was clear to me. I finally grew tired of the muddle. I wanted some clear place in my mind but could not find it, and could not find the quit of it either. Lord, I said, hold my hand will You, and help me sort this shit out.

I went fishing, threw my line into the dark. Nothing bit.

That night the air was dead thick hot and nearly unbreathable. Countless mosquitoes humming outside the bar. Moon tint on everything.

Just me and the fice. He is my buddy now. He kept looking at me like maybe I'll have some more pie for him soon.

Early Sunday morning I was scattering compost around an orange tree when the kid Lou Haden showed up. We walked the property.

This red-bark tree, he said, is a gumbo. He ran his hand along its peeling bark. They on the middens, nowhere else to speak of. I think the old Indians planted 'em, the mound builders. Maybe they had some meanin' we got no idea about now. You can cut off a stob, stick it in the ground and she'll start up. No need to fuss any. A moment later he said, I did have the thought once the midden was like a church in olden times, a place to worship. Do not know why that came to me without it happened to be a Sunday I was thinkin' on it.

I have wondered on that field out front too, he said. It is been worked a long time. I'd bet money the Seminoles planted corn there. You still see their pumpkins climbing the trees around the edge. But way back, it could be was for somethin' different entirely. Maybe for a game—

Like base-ball?

Prob'ly a might rougher, he said.

He put his hand on a young tree, seven-, eight-foot tall with wide, deep-green leaves. This is a alligator pear, he said. I planted seed pits when Lee and Emma got married. This an' another done well. They will make fruit in a year or two.

Point out Palma Sola to me, I said. I want to go over there.

He motioned toward the mouth of the river. When you rowin', look to this side o' the river. There's a single tall date palm along the shore. It stands out.

On this side? I said.

Yeh. Directly across from it is where you want.

A store is kept there?

Otis Pike's.

He has whiskey? I said.

He does. Good whiskey what I hear, and rum, too, tho' I never heard anybody talkin' up the rum. He is a religious feller but do not mind sellin' alcohol, even on the Lord's day. He is got a little open window to the side o' the store, a table and chairs settin' around under a big oak. Be careful tho', Lou said, he might cheat you, Christian or no. He may or may not. You jes' got to watch it.

I have heard that said.

The mangos are beddin' this moon. I fish at night, always catch a mess. You want to come along?

Mangos? I said.

Mango snappers. They's a spot I fish, has a rock pile down fifty feet or so. They like rocks. Long about dark, I'm in place and jes' stay there till I run out a bait.

I'll have to pass on it, I said.

Too bad, he said. They make fine table fare.

The rock pile, I said. You talkin' about limestone?

More likely granite. The big steamboats from up north, he said, they use rocks for ballast on the trip down and dump 'em when they get here. On the way back, they full o' timber and turpentine barrels and what all.

Before he left, Lou said, You might run into a old Neil Clary buddy over to Pike's—Linwood Scruggs. He drinks there most Sunday mornings. He lives close by us. My folks think him far gone peculiar, but ... he do not seem so out o' step to me. He always treated me straight up. You need to talk to 'im before he is been there too long tho'.

I rowed across. The river was calm then. Coming back would not be so easy.

I came to shore somewhat east of where I intended. I pulled into a little cove, just to sit and relax a bit, catch my breath. It was a pretty spot and nothing at all moving. In the boat, in this calm place on the river, the edge between sky and water vanished. They were some moments one, and I had the thought of being suspended in a still crossroad of the universe.

After a while I gathered myself and rowed on.

I pulled the boat up on shore alongside two others. There was a community of sorts, tho' not much of one. Pike's store was no more than a big shack. Acorns had sprouted in the cedar shakes, a good part of the roof rampant with Virginia creeper. The store proper was not open, but the side window was. There was a woman tending it. She looked to be Indian. I ordered whiskey, and she gave me a tin cup of it. I asked the price when I got the drink. She said the price, and I paid her. She understood the words whiskey and price, and I had the feeling that might have been it.

I had a look at the store goods. There were wide shelves along the back wall. Cornmeal, green coffee. Duke's Mixture chewing tobacco, snuff, cigars. Keg of nails ... gunpowder ... a good many whiskey jugs. Whiskey seemed to be the item here.

I took my cup to the table. A tall, lanky man sat there drinking, wore a slouch hat, butternut trousers, looked like maybe he had been wearing since the War ended. They did not have much time left. Galluses, no shirt. He sported a long blonde mustache. A double barrel shotgun leaned against the big live oak that shaded this side of the store, a bucket nearby with a cloth over the top the flies had some interest in.

Virgil, I said.
Linwood, he said.
What's in the bucket, Linwood?
Gator hide, he said.
I noticed his eyes then. I tried not to look at them again. They were dead. They were two hazel stones. He did not appear to be someone you'd want to get crosswise of, but he turned out to be an amiable sort.
You eat gator? I said.

I smoke the tail for dog food, he said. I'll trade that hide for my drinks today, or maybe it will be a partial payment.

Where's the owner? I hooked my thumb toward the store.

Otis? Sunday ... he is out in the woods prayin' for us sinners. Maybe gone convert some critters. Or checkin' on his still most likely. That is his wife. He do not mind her workin' on the Sabbath. Sunday the only time I come here, when he's not around and ever'body else is church meetin'.

The whiskey is good.

That it is, he said. I'll allow him that.

His wife Indian? I said.

Half blood. Cuban and Seminole. Once was a bunch of 'em around, when the Cubans had their fish camps goin'.

You the one workin' at the Mayfield place, he said after a bit. I seen you splittin' wood.

That would be me.

Folks around here think she is tetched, you know, still waitin' for Neil. Time ta piss on the fire an' call in the dogs on that.

You knew Neil?

Very well, he said. We both from here. He's from the north side the river, my family from over this way, on south a piece. The Clarys migrated from Massachusetts, but way back. Neil was born here. Got on from the time we was littl'uns.

Me and Neil ran herd for old man Sumerlin, he said, two years a that. It was our first real payin' job. When things went bad up north in '63, it wore at us. Tom Jackson got killed in May... sorry that star set. Seemed like things went downhill from there on. 'T were not long afore we questioned our part. Felt patriotic I guess. We were pretty sick a cow huntin' anyway.

Linwood shook his head slowly, got a pained expression. You could chuck two stones in the river for all the difference we made. '63 ... seems only yesterday, or maybe some other age, back in a gone time.

We went lookin' for the 7th Florida, he said. Did not even know where they were exactly, Tennessee or Georgia … or where the hell.

We left our catch-dogs with my folks. My first letter up there, I found out they ran a neighbor's cattle one night and got shot dead at it. Neil wanted ta bring 'em along. I should a listened.

Rode our little marsh tackies, had two apiece. A good pack mule. We took our sweet time. It all jes' seemed a lark. The trip went on about forever. We had no idea how far Tennessee was. It tested our idea a distance. An' only fools' luck we made it there safe. One a Neil's ponies gave out early on, got the staggers. Then one a mine got sorely worsted near Atlanta, saddle-galled so bad I turned him loose. Neil's other was lame by the time we got up there, and he went infantry. My horse was iron-legged an' the orneriest I ever owned. He made it jes' on account a his meanness.

I got assigned as a courier. I could ride my ass off. There was some excitement in the job. I done tolerable well at it. I did not see Neil all that much … saw him when I could. Were you in? Maybe you too young.

I told him about the fight at Natural Bridge.

So you were in the War two days?

Yeh.

You got the picture I would think, he said.

Does not sound like you believe Neil is comin' back, I said.

Well, no … 'spect not. The army had him down as *Missing*. No one saw him get busted up. That he'd surrendered to the Yanks, that did not enter my mind. I think he'd jack-knife into his grave 'fore he'd do such a thing. No one saw him walk off either, or … if they had, they were shut-mouthed about it. But I think that is what he did. A whole lot a boys lit out toward the end there in Atlanta. An' were not a man jack amongst 'em did not think on it. Now what befell him after he walked, who knows?

When John Bell Hood took over up there, he said, it all went ta shit. He was good at openin' hell's gate. He did that well enough. He only knew ta close it by stackin' up the dead.

Miss Mayfield says he has a home in New Orleans, I said.

That is a far cry from how it ought a be. An' too bad. I had ev'ry intention a pissin' on his grave, could I found it. What say you?

About what?

Neil makin' it home.

No opinion, I said. Can I buy you a whiskey?

Sho.

Would you tell me some what he was like?

Neil? Linwood Scruggs smiled. He was a rascal.

I'll tell you, those eyes and that smile made strange partners.

I went and ordered two whiskeys.

We drank some, looked around, relaxed. It was a slow and easy sort of day. He spoke of the War: I went through three horses up there. The first two found early graves from bad grub and rough travel. Did not get enough grain. Livin' on grass and not much a that when the weather set in cold. The last one got shot out from under me, air blowin' out frost from a hole in her chest. I hated that I lost her. She could run. She was steadfast in a fight. Ill fortune for me. Not so good for her either.

The army had nothin' left but crowbait by then, used up horses what needed condemned. I picked out one hack and rode him for a day. The next mornin' the old feller could hardly walk he was so stiff ... an' so I became infantry.

Now I was not used ta footin' it. My first march was but 10 miles. The boys around me came in game, counted it an easy day. I'd drawed some new, low-quarter shoes when we was encamped at Florence, Alabama. I had those all a two days, an' some asshole stole 'em.

I was hopin' Florence would be our winter quarters. I wanted some idle time. Pitchin' horseshoes. Checkers. Maybe a whiskey ration throwed in the bargain. But then Hood came up with one a his plans, an' we hit the road again. We left Florence in November in bitter weather. I mean we all like to a froze. Rumor had it we was Nashville bound. So now I'm barefoot ... no matter it's ice an' snow on the ground ... built entrenchments when we got where we were goin' ... very seldom even the least notion why we stopped where we had. Picket detail at night now and then for an extra treat. Eatin' field peas an' pickled hog ... sometimes half rations ... sometimes naught. Makin' do on black walnuts.

I ate my belt. A part anyway. Did not need it all, I had gone so skinny. Fried it up with a little pork fat ... not half bad. A bit chewy. March some more, on to some place we knew not of. Fight. Get our ass kicked. I was lookin' for somebody would accept my surrender.

I recall the fights clearly, he said. Ever' one. An' I wish it otherwise. I recall bein' eat up with lice. Doubt they will make the hist'ry books—the nits and lice.

I never was wounded. I jes' give out. My legs below the knee felt like wood. I was poorly, I'll tell ye. Felt like I been shook over hell. When we marched I kept an eye on my feet so I'd know where they were. The boys from there said it was the worst winter they ever known.

This one evenin', we was close on Nashville by then, gittin' there anyway, I went to visit old friends encamped nearby. They were artillery, belonged ta Hoxton's Battalion. Florida boys. From up around Perry. One, Stedman Givens, was my cousin. They were takin' supper and offered me a portion—raw pork, froze hard as stone. No fires allowed ta be kindled that night. Was nobody callin' out for seconds. You jes' got it down best you could. An' we sat there, huddled around a wood stack that would not be lit till morning, makin' warmth out a friendship an' talk.

Now I said we were close on Nashville, but it was only a guess. No one much knew where we were. Talked about that some. How this campaign so far, we could not seem to locate ourselves. Discussed, like most always, what might be in store for us when the War was done. It's all we cared about then ... was goin' home ... preferably in one piece. The War was well along. It was gone run its course. We had a pretty good idea it would not end well. An' then what? Would the Yanks let us mosey on home then? We doubted they would sweeten it for us any. Talked about how scarce rumors were in camp of late. No mail. The only news at all came from Yankee pickets we talked with. There were always a good many rumors about. You could not credit them, but you listened. Right then, there was only one makin' the rounds, an' it made such little sense it was likely true. After General Hood kicked ass in Nashville, it went, he wanted to take on Ohio next. Go conquer Cincinnati or some shit. This in the dead a winter mind you. That got us amused. An' we talked about Florida sunshine, what we'd give for a canteen a whiskey, an' ... You know, I can see us settin' there in my mind right now, some scarecrow johnny rebs to be sure, but sanguine even so.

An' one by one went high-steppin' into the bushes. We'd come back, an' shortly high-step it again. We all had the shits so bad an' out a sorts in other ways more'n you could count ... an' it became hilarious. I mean, you had ta laugh sometimes or the damn mis'ry would kill you outright.

Was not but two days later I helped load some a them boys into an ambulance for their last ride.

I'd been on picket all night, a mile from camp, mile an' a half. A bad night, the snow spittin'. There was Yank pickets across from us, but they were not up for any trouble an' we returned the favor. We got relieved at first light an' headed back. We was all but there when a shell passed overhead an' exploded in camp. One a them lone, here I come a-knockin' shells. See if anybody's home. Two boys was gone already. Four others jes' fucked, cousin Stedman amongst 'em.

You were forbidden to help wounded off the field lest you was ambulance cor'. I could not work up enough give-a-shit by then. I rode along an' cared for 'em … did what I could. It was a mess in that wagon … looked like a butcher been at 'em with his meat axe. We bounced along ta the field hospital, scatterin' crows all the way. One a them boys survived, what I heard. You never knew about that. Some lived through shit you could not believe they made it.

Stedman did not make it. He is still there, camped across the Dark River.

All I saw up there, an' that ride is two-bits a scenery I can not shake. It travels in my mind still.

The next day, we had a brush with the Yanks near a village called Spring Hill, an' that was it for me. You ever been sun struck bad? That's what it felt like, at first anyway. Then it got worse. When I give out, what they tell me … I took ta walkin' in circles, starin' hard at the ground. What you think I was lookin' for there?

I came around at a hospital, way in the rear. No idea how I got there. Franklin was the next stop for my outfit, 13 miles north a Spring Hill. Thank God I did not make it there or you'd be talkin' with my ghost.

An' pretty much, Linwood added, I been crazy ever since.

He smiled again.

Dang! I thought. That is eerie.

They put me on extended leave, he said. I thought they'd muster me out, cashier me … whatever they do with head cases … but I never heard a thing from 'em. An' then the War was over.

We drank to that.

He spoke of Neil Clary and Ella Mayfield:

It was a sight, he said. Here come Ella out a the blue from New Orleans, cast a sidelong pretty look at Neil, and he bit. 'T were not like him, gettin' hooked so. His life slanted some different 'fore she come around.

He had girls from here ta Georgia ... all different colors ... never cared a damn about 'em, one way or t'other, that I could tell. A rough woman, a pretty one, skinny, or well-favored, no matter. He acted like there was this goin' out a bidness sale at a whorehouse.

An' he was bad at leavin' out the back door with a husband or boyfriend walkin' in the front. The one-eyed dummy ruled that kingdom.

Neil was good with his fists, an' at times had ta be. He was not one you'd trifle with. He had violent hands.

An' it all changed with a look. That madcap shit a his up an' left. I was hard put understandin' it. Was not till I spent time around Ella that I caught on.

Neil took it hard leavin' her, but he did what he felt right. We all did. You as well.

I was there when they said their goodbyes. They both of 'em nigh fell apart. I went an' had a conversation with our mule for a while.

Were they married? I said. She sometimes speaks that way. That she is Neil's wife.

Not preacher married, Linwood said.

I visited her some since the War, he said. Bein' around her can lighten your step. She is well-knit ... and fair ... and that's not even it. That blame gal can get ta playin' on your heartstrings. She ain't tryin', do not even know it. But you can not help fallin' for her.

I know what you mean, I said.

We caroused many hours there at the table in the shade, drinking and sweating and trading stories. I asked at one point if he knew Jonah Coyle.

The poltroon? he said. And had no other comment on the subject.

You know, Linwood said after awhile, you best get a move on. The tide is a-changin'. It is headed out. Might be a hard row here directly.

I had half a drink left and sat around there to finish it, which turned out to be a mistake. Was not until I stood to leave that I realized I was smoked.

It took some time to get back across. I made it about half the way, ran into a heavy chop on the water, and began pullin' on the oars like mad but stayed in place. The chop just slapped the boat. There were pelicans diving for fish around me. I guess the boat offered the fish some shade, it being nearly stationary and all. But the effort sobered me. I got a second wind. I finally made it across up near the mouth of the river. There was a real possibility for a while I was going to shoot on out into the Gulf and maybe see the world. I pulled the boat way up on shore, I would retrieve it in the morning, and walked back to the midden. Near sunset by then, blue sky, yellow clouds.

The women returned at noon Monday. I had retrieved the boat and did not mention the rowing competition I'd nearly lost. Scallops were ripe for picking in the grass flats, and I had gathered a half bucket for us to eat.

Miss Mayfield wanted to tell me all about their visit. I set about cleaning scallops as she spoke.

She had come back with a novel Coyle's mother had loaned her, *The Mill on the Floss*. She was excited about that. There had been a grand horse race, with little black boys in different colored bandannas as jockeys. Jonah Coyle had loaned Miss Mayfield some money to make a wager, and she won.

I noticed Sugarbee knit her brow on that.

We have enough money for the downspout now, the gutters, she said.

There were musicians, she went on. A fiddler and a gourd banjo and a squeezebox.

He sawin' away, Sugarbee said. Make a fiddle tawk.

An' one fella was a whistler.

'T was sweet, Sugarbee said.

The negroes put on cock fights. Sug liked that. I did not care for it so much, she said. We sang around a big bonfire on the 4th. *Annie Laurie, Lorena, Jimmy Long Josey*, all those old good songs. It was fun, Virgil. Shoot ... I wish you had come along.

Sure, too bad, I thought. I sing like a hound dog on a porch.

There had been company from Havana, she said, the Cosgrove family, once upon a time from Grenada, Mississippi. These folks were related to Coyle, the woman a first cousin. Her name was Melissa tho' they called her Mel. Her husband went by Coot. The couple and their five young boys were visiting to escape the Yella Jack, bad in Cuba just then. A neighbor there the Cosgroves befriended, a Confederate woman from South Carolina, had come down with it and soon after perished.

She ran all that by me in a hurry, excited by the telling or maybe sensed that I was indifferent. I did not give a red cent. I could not even play like I cared.

Dem keeds, Sugarbee said, all look alike.

Miss Mayfield agreed. And I never could get their names straight. They was all had Bible names.

She showed me two beeswax candles she brought back. The children had been dipping candles. Here, smell ...

Faint odor of honey.

Mr. Coyle, she said, had what he called butter whiskey from Kentucky. That was good. And we ate till we hurt ourselves.

What are Confederates doin' in Havana? I said. It was not the smartest question, I realized, but not until it had already escaped me. Her expression changed, the question had nettled her, but she started to answer in such a civil way, it made me realize my own civility and manners were lacking.

I said something wrong, I said. Forgive me. I do not want to be a botherment to you, ever.

I know that, Virgil. It ... just ... they plain can not deal with that we lost the War.

They are shunning their home?

I do not know as they would put it that way. They think of Mississippi as subjugated country. They are in exile. Mr. Coyle said there are Confederates in Mexico, too, little colonies of them around. In Brazil—

A cloud of ibis passed overhead just then, and we all looked skyward.

Sugarbee saved me from saying anything else dumb.

Dey a mans livin' in a rum barrel, she said.

He is not living in it, Miss Mayfield said. For goodness sake. He's dead. They are waiting for a schooner to take him up to New York for burial, she explained to me. He had been a good friend of Coyle's folks.

He is keeping in a barrel of rum? I said.

Yes, she said. He is a pickle by now I guess. She did her quick little side smile. I am so sorry, she said. That is not funny.

Then she laughed with abandon.

Sugarbee turned her head and looked at me.

Miss Mayfield recovered her senses at length.

Sug refused to go near that barrel, she went on. You should seen her give that barrel a wide berth. Would not even look directly upon it.

I ain't like to stare at such, Sugarbee said. 'T is seedy.

They learned at Coyle's that Florida had been readmitted to the Union the previous month.

I told Miss Mayfield about meeting Linwood Scruggs.
That boy's a pistol, she said. Him and Neil, those two did some caperin' in the old days. Tho' neither would admit that to me, just angels on the loose, to hear them tell it.
That smile a his, I said.
Yes, she said. He has bad teeth.
Yeh, that, I said. But what I meant was, when combined with those eyes—
He looks like a killer? you mean. He does. Or some ugly customer at least. He's a sweetheart, tho'. He did not return from the War altogether sound. He had a hard time getting back on board ...
She spoke a bit more but appeared to run out of spark in the process.
Then, and I guess for the first time, it was hard to make conversation with her. We looked at each other a moment or two longer. There seemed nothing left to say to one another. She walked away suddenly toward the house, she had to rest she told us.
Sug ... would you fix Virgil something to eat.
How 'bout you? Sugarbee said.
She went into the house without answering.

Sugarbee grilled the scallops on cedar skewers. In four, five minutes they were done perfectly. We ate.
Many folks there? I said.
Ev'ry bukrah from miles aroun'. Not ary a one, fancy or po, more'n a bumpkin dat I could tell. Jes' hicks.
I asked about the horse race where Miss Mayfield won money.
Fixed, she said. Marse Coyle want her to win. She made a dismissive sound. Marse. Hit what his niggers call 'im. Like back in olden days. He rich as cream, own a whole world o' land, but he ain't got no mistis ... an' be around 'im you see f'why. He twitchy as a squirrel. Anyways ...

Ole Coyle nod to his Boss nigger, an' he go tawk to the li'l boys ridin'. An' her win. No reason other wise. Dat hoss o' hers a nag. A ol' plug.

She all right? I said.

Sometime, wit fun ... afterward her blues come.

I looked away.

You musant be cross wit' her, she said. Stop bein' so sulky. You in de pouts.

She got back onto Jonah Coyle.

You 'member when he come heh? How he axt all statue-y, nigh stiffern a board? Hit what he do to hold back de twitchin'.

I got to grinning some.

Now take you. You's nigh asleep aroun' her.

What? I am not, I said.

But Coyle, now, he a pester. Her jes' want to git shut o' him.

There were lightning chains over the Gulf that evening, and squalls moved in on us. The rain still came down a little when Sugarbee woke me in the morning. A redbird sang nearby, and a mate answered.

Virgil.

Yes'm.

Dat wind las' night messed wit me.

What happened?

Dere a big limb down, out'n my melons. An' I stumped my foot kickin' at 'im.

It's rainin', I said.

You made out o' sugar? she said. C'mon. Coffee ready.

I took the broadaxe.

Look, I said. I had taken care of the limb and moved the cut wood off to the side of the garden. I am fixin' to leave here soon. I need to go home.

You were not often going to surprise her, no matter

what you told her.

We stood in the rain. She studied me.

When? she said.

I'm workin' on a kitchen cord for you. When I finish, I'll stack the wood up by the house. I want to get that done. I have to go to the village here shortly and check on transportation. Might be awhile afore I get out. Might not.

She shook her head *yes* slightly. She said, I need to tend my truck-patch, and left me standing there.

I was out by the wood piles along the shore later on when Miss Mayfield came up to me. The rain had stopped.

Take a walk with me in the water, she said.

I rolled up my pant legs.

We walked the fiddler flats toward the west. The water temperature of late felt close to a warm bath.

Sug says you leavin'.

Yes, I said.

She took my hand. We walked a long way holding hands, and it seemed a most natural thing.

I want you to go home, she said, and then I want you to think on comin' back.

I have work to do at the farm, I said. We'll get busy soon.

Will you be free by Christmas? she said. Not Christmas itself. I know you want to be with your family then. But after? Daddy sends me money at Christmas time. I can pay you for the work you done.

I have been paid, I said.

She stopped walking, turned, and kissed me on the cheek.

She smiled.

Think about it, she said.

I will.

Promise?

Yes.

She kissed me again and after said, You need not look

so astounded.

Where have we got to here? I said.

Some place close I think, she said.

What about Jonah Coyle?

What about him? She touched my hair. Need a haircut you goin' home, she said. You are lookin' wild, boy.

We walked some more.

At one point I told her: I like you right well.

It is hard to understand how five words could behave so halting and tongue-tied as those did. But at least I said it.

A pair of rays glided by us in the river. Sug calls them stingerees, she said.

I had the strangest dream last night. I thought it time to go to sleep, she said, but there was an empty spot where my bed sets. I went and got Sug. She came into the house and said, What chu do wit' yer bed? talking just how she does. No idea, I told her. I guess I misplaced it.

I wonder what that amounted to?

You got me, she said. And it was one of those dreams where you are right there moving about and making conversation, and all of it so real. I mean, how do you go about losing a bed?

We need to turn around, she said a moment later. I swear ... I am just not feeling right. I do not feel myself.

I need to go to the village, I said, see about a ride out. Not sure what might be available.

When you get back, she said, I'll trim your hair.

Gulls up ahead of us were laughing.

I rowed the boat to Manatee. It was hot out, and a long hot ride, the river still, the air. The village looked deserted. I saw no white people, not a one. Nor a soul working at the wharf. There was a small steamboat moored there, the gangway plank hauled in, but no movement aboard. I stopped a negro who was leading a black horse down the

shoreline.
　Where is everyone?
　Gone, he said. O stayin' inside. Be Yella Jack at Coyle's.

　When I got back to the midden, Sugarbee was washing the shirt Miss Mayfield had on that morning.
　Her nose start bleedin', she said. Her crine. Her never cry—
　There is fever at Coyle's farm, I said.
　Oh no ... Oh Lawd. Pray to Mary, no. Mon bon Dieu ...
　When she had gathered herself she said, Go see Otis Pike. She handed me an empty jug. Git dis filled wit' whiskey. You still got dat money o' yourn?
　I had enough to get home. I had extra.
　Sure, I said. The whiskey for her?
　No, she said. Us. Dis ain't gone be pretty. Not by a long shot. Fetch coffee beans. Some stick candy. He got horehound candy. Maybe peppermints. An' seegars ... boo-coo.
　You thirsty for tobacco? I said.
　Jack doan like smoke, she said. Paregoric, too, dere be any.
　What's that?
　Dope, she said. Now hasten.

　Otis Pike turned out to be a big man, pick-axe nose, round head, bull neck. He had cropped hair like a convict and an ear trumpet. News had traveled. He would not get close to me.
　I recognize the boat. You got the sickness o'er there? He put the trumpet to his ear.
　Yes, I said. Miss Mayfield.
　I'll pray for her, he said. What you want?
　He had me to wait out in the yard while he filled the order. He would not touch our whiskey jug, told me to take it back. He replaced it with one of his own. He set the items down on the table outside then and backed away. He would

not accept my money either but said he would put it all on Miss Mayfield's charge.

She has a charge?

She do now, he said.

You got a yaller cloth or some such, hang it out front by the water, stop folks from come wanderin' up, not knowin'. God bless, he said, and I left.

Crossing the river, I felt like I was rowing uphill. I handed over the supplies to Sugarbee back at the midden.

No paregoric, I said.

She took a cigar and lit it.

Her lookin' paper-y, she said.

Miss Mayfield was burning and shivering by turns. She had a headache. She ran a finger across the middle of her forehead.

It hurts right there, she said. A straight line of hurt.

Sugarbee was sprinkling brine on the floor of the house.

What is that do?

Not sarten. I seen Ol' Auntie do hit.

Your aunt?

No. Be her name. Ol' Auntie.

Her a conj'in woman, Sugarbee said, gone now, a long many years. A treater. Her woyked de roots and yarbs. Den her turn old an' inclined to religion, put her past away. An' de Holy Spirit showed up one day in her touch.

Yarbs?

As I had not intended to say that, I guess I wondered it out loud.

Sugarbee turned and gave me a look.

Quit yer fooleries now, she said.

When Miss Mayfield started retching, Sugarbee shooed me outside. I walked the midden. I went down to the river. I watched three dolphin in the grass flats, in water maybe nine foot deep, encircle a small school of mackerel, round them up into a ball and dart through it feeding.

I had a strong desire to do chores, to work at them ardently in a mindless way. But I went to the woodpile and could not get to it. I looked at the river. It looked back with uncountable blinking eyes. Everything still, but for the low, continuous, back and forth of the river as it swang against the shoreline, a slight wind blowing, the leaf and shadow dance. There is something in all that I have noticed many times now—another rhythm your body gets to following. I was taken by it a moment or two. And just as quickly back to where I started from.

When I returned to the house, Miss Mayfield was sleeping.

Her heart ain't got a good stroke, Sugarbee said. Her swounded.

She fainted?

Twicet. I had a hard time bring her to.

I'm worried about her, I said.

In two days, she said, Miss Ella gone right hersef ... or be a whole lot woyse.

The next two mornings, early on, there were storms far out in the Gulf, lightning prancing about, and a coolness in the breeze that came to us. Each day a rainbow in the west. Sugarbee killed and dressed three guinea hens and made soup in her long-legged kettle, let it simmer. She included a good dose of salt. Greens. Onions. Dimba leaves. She called it fever brew.

She fed the broth to Miss Mayfield. She put sweet potatoes on the embers to cook at night so the next morning they would be warm and ready to eat. That is what the two of us ate, potatoes and hen. And we had a drink of Pike's whiskey now and again.

On the second day at noon as we were having one such drink on the porch, a little screech owl landed on the rocking chair, sat observing us.

What is he up to? I said.

I doan like hit, she said. Be a token from de wrong side.

Miss Mayfield suffered without complaint, but she looked wrung out. Her face was flushed, a purple cast to her cheekbones, upper lip swollen. Her hair lank.

Look at my tongue, she said.

She stuck out her tongue. It was pure white.

I helped Sugarbee wash clothes and bedding. I rinsed them in the river first. Sugarbee set cistern water to boiling, her wash tubs placed near the kitchen fires. She took lye soap to the clothes and bedding in one tub, knocked them senseless with her battling stick, then rinsed them in another, her hands turning red at it. Then I hung what she gave me to dry.

I was idly checking Otis Pike's bill to see if it was correct. I was watching Sugarbee taking clothes off the line. I can cipher well enough. There are not that many things I need to add up. And yet this woman came to far more than what I had first estimated.

The physicians of the day, according Doc Bigbie, did little more than experiment on their yellow fever patients.

One of the oldest of verities, Doc said. If it is not possible to find cause nor cure to a sickness, put your trust in alchemy.

They prescribed quinine, its value confirmed, at least in other instances. Laudanum, a tincture of opium and saffron. Gave them doses of calomel, which was but mercury that burned holes in their stomachs. They were scarifiers, bled and cupped their patients. They sometimes hired barbers to do their bloodletting. They had traded in leeches for the barbers not long past. But they themselves heated glass cups, then placed them on the skin, that broke the blood vessels beneath and caused blistering. Rubbed them down violently with spirits of turpentine. Used mustard plasters.

Any way they could irritate the skin seemed of importance somehow. When none of that worked, they administered Dover's Powder, which contained opium, and antimony to enhance the effects. They might then finish their treatment with a solution of arsenic.

If the disease did not kill you, the remedy surely might. Truth to tell, it seemed God's will if you made it through and the devil's if not.

The first killing frost was the only thing that stopped it, and no one knew why that was so either.

Not a spoonful o' sense, Sugarbee said. What yer mama give you?

Castor oil and turpentine, I guess. It's what she prescribed no matter what.

I mixt castor oil wit ash an' water to help her stomach ache. Auntie call hit soot tea.

Sugarbee went on … she said Ol' Auntie's treatment for the sickness had been broth, soot tea and coffee, sponge baths, as she had the novel idea that comfort helped. That she put her hands on the ailing, offered up silent prayer. That she told Bible stories, and thought them a kind of medicine.

I meant to ask if any of that worked, but thought I might not like the answer.

Sugarbee had me get stick candy just because Miss Mayfield liked it. She sucked on the candy now and then. She got down a little broth. If you mentioned food, she made a face.

Sugarbee took to praying at odd moments, speaking aloud to her bon Dieu. She steady-on had a cigar in her mouth, eyes squinted against the smoke.

By the third morning, Ella Mayfield's face had turned yellow.

Sugarbee said to me, Her beyond mendin' now.

Sugarbee and I stood by the fire pit that held her long-legged kettle. The coals underneath it were ash. She lifted the lid. There was nothing left but char on the bottom of the pot.

We'll make do, I said.

No, she said. Tonight we sup on our cup o' sorrow.

Toward the end, when Miss Mayfield's stomach was on fire and she began vomiting black, she stayed completely sensible, her mind steady.

I stood by the river looking toward the west. There was a dark tempest brewing in the Gulf, a mighty cloud-rack there, a cross thunder. Lightning made the air white-veined. The sky looked to be cracking.

I went to the house and found Miss Mayfield sitting up on the side of her bed. I sat next to her. I put my hand around her wrist and could barely feel her heart. She wore a muslin shimmy. But for her Sunday best, it was about all she had left at the moment. Her other clothes were drying and not at all quick about it for the weather.

It stinks terrible in here, she said.

She put her hands to her stomach.

My in'ards, she said, feel like I ate glass.

She leaned her head on my shoulder.

Aw, Sam Hell, I thought.

The wind got up. The oak trees around the house were shaken. The chair on the porch started rocking.

I told her everything then. I put Neil's ring into her hand and closed her hand around it, said of how I came to have it and why I kept my secret. It was a secret not meant to be, but got to be, I said, an' I am sorry now it happened so.

I spoke of my time with Neil Clary, what of that time I could recall just then. I was in a hurry. I said it all so quickly, but she had already gone to be with him.

    Sugarbee went down to the river and blew her conch shell. She kept at it, hammered a death-song into the sky. Her guinea hens gathered about. The fice went howling into the woods, fast along a trail that seemed no more than smoke. The little steamboat I had noticed moored at the village passed by headed west and tolled its bell. And then it was all behind me and, as is the way of time, suddenly in the long ago and days of old.

1900
The Lake House,
Mount Dora, Florida
Spring

    I have lived at this hotel the past two years. I brought a few clothes from home, my Colt pistol, Bowie knife, spittoon. Folks stay here awhile, they leave. I get to know them or not. It works for me either way. The owner has a pet rooster that smokes cigarettes. That's about it for fancy entertainment.

    I would like to tell you about what happened on the lake this morning. The sky was gray. Wells of sunlight angled down through the cloud cover now and again, an antique yellow to them. I was in my row boat, fishing. And I caught a nice bass. This only happens by accident anymore, as I pay no attention to my line. I am going to say the fish weighed close to nine pounds, and you can believe me or not.

    I let it go. She swam away very slow, contemplating her luck possibly. Have you ever noticed there are instances when one thing has nothing to do with another, and yet it does. By some odd valence of memory, that fish moving off like it did made everything kind of lazy and many years ago. Old friends gathered round.

    The likes of Neil Clary and Ella Mayfield did not come my way again. They were once and once only.

    They have been joined by others who I see no longer, but—tho' that time when we were young is no more than an echo now—those two do not change. They live on in me just as they were.

    I have had a long life. Long enough. I had not the least

expectation of it. I would fain record that it was an original life. It was not. It was unassuming and gentle as I could keep it.

I had taken to the notion back then that everyone died young. You are here, then gone, and that is the way of it. Why they left so early and I carried on, there is no getting a purchase to. You can spend your mind at it, and render nothing. I never told their story before, the tracks they left on this hard earth, not to anyone no matter how close. I kept them secret.

I do not much belong in this new century. My inclination is to step back from it. I have tired lately of this world and started to look beyond. I witnessed in the fallen at Natural Bridge that the body is no anchor to the soul. It sails on. I believe now that the soul is a great explorer.

I have taken due measure of this world, so that in the next I can look back and not be afraid to let go.

I have noted lately that a man grows old yet his dreams do not age. I will follow them soon I can tell. I can nearly make them out now of an evening, toward the west, waiting for me down where the road bends.

In telling this story, I received invaluable help from a number of works, especially these:

- *The Battle of Natural Bridge, Florida: The Confederate Defense of Tallahassee*, by Dale Cox
- *Edge of Wilderness: A Settlement History of Manatee River and Sarasota Bay*, by Janet Snyder Matthews
- *Brokenburn: The Journal of Kate Stone 1861-1868*, edited by John Q. Anderson
- *William McLeod Diary.* Florida Memory. Civil War Voices of Florida
- *Far from Fields of Glory–Military Operations in Florida During the Civil War 1864-1865*, by David James Coles. A doctoral dissertation FSU 1996
- *The Red Hills of Florida*, by Clifton Paisley
- *Yellow Fever and the South*, by Margaret Humphreys
- *One Hundred Years in Palmetto, Florida*, by Ruth E. Abel
- *Company Aytch*, by Sam Watkins
- *Through Some Eventful Years*, by Susan Bradford Eppes
- *Rebel Unknown* tintype from E.T.M. Collectibles, Danville PA

And a note of respect for Robert and Anna Webb Griffith, Manatee River pioneers

Tom Abrams lives in Florida. This is his third novel. His story collection, *The Drinking of Spirits*, was reviewed favorably in *Publishers Weekly*.